S0-BBF-278

LOCOMOTION

LOCOMOTION

Elizabeth Evans

Minnesota Voices Project Number 23

New Rivers Press 1986

Library of Congress Catalog Card Number: 85-06849
ISBN 0-89823-071-3
Book Design: Gaylord Schanilec
Typesetting: Peregrine Cold Type

Many of these stories (some in slightly different form) have appeared in the
following publications: *Appearances, Black Warrior Review, Kalliope,
Crazyhorse, Cimarron Review*, and *Mademoiselle*. Our thanks to the editors of
these publications for permission to reprint here. Front cover painting by
Elizabeth Evans.

Locomotion has been published with the aid of grant support from the Jerome
Foundation, the First Bank System Foundation, the McKnight Foundation, and
the United Arts Council (with special assistance from the McKnight Foundation),
and the National Endowment for the Arts (with funds appropriated by the
Congress of the United States).

New Rivers Press books are distributed by

Bookslinger	and	Small Press Distribution, Inc.
213 East 4th St.		1814 San Pablo Ave.
St. Paul, MN		Berkeley, CA
55101		94702

Locomotion has been manufactured in the United States of America for New
Rivers Press, Inc. (C. W. Truesdale, editor/publisher), 1602 Selby Ave., St. Paul,
MN 55104 in a first edition of 1,000 copies.

For Steve

LOCOMOTION

THE SLEEPING GYPSY

Dorothy Debbins palms her shoulder-length hair back from her face. This is a gesture she picked up at the movies, watching Katherine Hepburn, Barbara Stanwyck, and Bette Davis; but now, some thirty plus years after the fact, instead of being off-handedly provocative, it is her sign of weariness and dismay.

The dismay comes in part from the fact that she is having a South Seas party this evening (bubbling fountains are making their way across town to her door, flowers are losing their heads in the big florist shop, a vacuum whirs down the Persian runner in the front hall), yet Dorothy's daughter sits in the den circling possible jobs in the want ads with a blue highlighter.

Dorothy picks up several pages of newsprint which Alice has dropped on the creamy carpeting. She loves her daughter dearly, *dearly*. I'd cut off my right arm for her, she often protests, but she hates to see Alice sitting like that, eating peanut butter from the jar, her bathrobe still on at noon, her long blond hair badly in need of washing. The girl refuses to answer the phone and has instructed her parents to tell all callers that she is "out." Whenever Dorothy asks what is wrong, Alice makes jokes: "I vant to be alone," she says with a vampire's smile, and, yesterday, "Just waiting for my prince to come, Ma." Ma. The girl thought that was funny, too.

It has been three months since Alice abandoned college, showed up on the Debbins' front steps, laughing, scrawny in an enormous full-length formal that was straight from Goodwill. Dorothy has to agree with Martin when he says Alice must have *worked* to schedule so many courses (The Detective in Contemporary Novels, Theater of Communion, Cowboys and Indians in American Film) which taught nothing in the way of employable skills.

"Dear," Dorothy says on a sudden inspiration. She drops an afghan on that piece of her daughter's foot which sticks out from beneath the bathrobe. "You could do me a big favor by running over to that import place we drove by last week. Marybeth says they have the candles for the torches there."

Alice glances up from the newspaper and out the window as if she has heard a distant strain of music. "Look at that!" she says, and points to a squirrel tight-roping its way across a section of telephone wire. "Hello to you, too!" she says to the squirrel when it shakes its plumed tail.

Dorothy removes her eye glasses, taps the bow against her front teeth. "Do you think you could do that for me?" she asks. Alice nods and makes a blue question mark next to an item in the paper. "You'll have to get going soon, though," Dorothy says. "I'll treat you to lunch out, too. Why don't you call Delia Stuart and ask her along?"

"Delia?" Alice says with a snort. She stretches newly chubby arms forward, hands together, a child preparing for a dive. "Delia!" She laughs.

After Alice is gone, greasy hair pulled back from her pretty face with a shoestring, Dorothy looks at the want ads. Alice has marked as possibilities: a cocktail waitress opening at a Holiday Inn, sorter at McCormick's, and something called a "gluer." Gad. Dorothy's friends' daughters might reject the graces of a home, but at least they become lawyers and designers and editors at publishing houses, enter a world of attractive efficiency, three piece suits, elevators whooshing up to a carpeted office, men leaning over desks. Most of them marry eventually. They give parties which their parents are happy to attend. They send cracker-thick christening announcements to Dorothy and Martin, take up so completely the life Dorothy intended for Alice that sometimes she feels as if she has been robbed.

* * *

Exquisitely angular arrangement of Bird of Paradise between them, Dorothy and Martin sit at the dining room table. Dorothy helps herself to a cup of coffee and a croissant. The roll is buttery and good and by the time she's finished chewing her first bite, she's thinking ahead to the possibility of a second roll, which she *cannot* afford, since she's vowed to get out of size sixteen by the boys' Thanksgiving visit. She sighs and pushes two of the croissants off to the side of the platter for Lorna's coffee break.

Martin clears his throat. "Our little gathering was quite a success," he says.

"I think so, too," says Dorothy, pleased his assessment matches hers. "That's the first time in quite a while that everyone's stayed out 'til three!" Which made them feel young and carefree, not at all like grandparents and people who were starting to make more and more trips to the hospital for tests, surgical procedures, heart attacks. Dorothy danced a hula; they put on the old Dorsey records and, cheek to cheek, she and Martin moved across the living room's parquet floor. But something is off, eludes her, as if she is trying to remember a person or a song and all she has to go on is the hem of a coat moving out the door, one note. Then, plain as those terrible falls at night, in bed and half asleep, she feels something drop — she is empty below her breasts and above her thighs — and there it is, Harold Traccig, who gave Alice an interview at his paper products firm, Harold pecking Dorothy on the cheek last night and saying of Alice, "She's a heck of a sharp girl, whew! She's going to get her head screwed on one of these days and, then, look out world!" Complicit. Friendly. As if he assumed Dorothy would understand what he meant. Just like the first night Alice was home from college for good, and, a little drunk from Martin's wine pushing, the girl said, calm, matter of fact, "Admit it, Dorothy, you're miserable." Then, Dorothy was so surprised, so hurt at being that misunderstood, all she could do was find some small smile for her face and say, before Martin started yelling at the girl, "I don't remember you ever calling me Dorothy before."

Dorothy spreads apricot jam on her croissant. So. Alice. Dorothy thinks of the girl scrambling over the rocks at the cabin, skinny, showing a mouthful

10

of braces, practicing the piano with long fingers carefully bent above the keyboard, wearing the fuzz off the head of her Ken doll with the kissing of Barbie. It was Alice who stayed by Dorothy's bed when Dorothy used to have her migraines. Lorna reminded Dorothy of it just the other day, how Alice bobbypinned a napkin to her head — a little nurse-waitress — and made Dorothy sugary lemonade with cracked ice. Alice pressed cool cloths to Dorothy's forehead while Dorothy hung, ill, over the toilet bowl. She read her mother fairy tales, made Dorothy smile with her queer interpretations: "Cinderella" and "Snow White," Alice said, were stories about how it was important your mother didn't die. "The *sweetest* child," Lorna said, almost tearful, "and now she won't *talk* to me!" Teachers put the mentally retarded students next to Alice because, they told Dorothy, the girl was so kind. She was their best student, they said. While Alice's brothers were accused of things that made Dorothy weep with shame and disbelief (shooting a farmer's cow and dog, cheating on the SAT, breaking into a house): yet now they are both lawyers, married, with a child apiece, and Alice —

Alice sits on the floor with her old rock collection, matching the cleaved faces of stones with dull exteriors, glittering insides.

After Alice's last failed romance, the girl's oldest brother told Dorothy over the phone, "When it comes to falling in love, she's like a diabetic with sugar or something; she can't handle that, you know?"

Dorothy did not know how to answer. The girl does not seem to have even girl friends anymore. The only indications of college pals have been a phone call which Dorothy connected to Alice's request for a five hundred dollar "loan," and a sign hung on Alice's doorknob. "Closet," the sign reads, imperative as a Do Not Disturb. Alice explained that some girls left it on her knob at school after the dorm's custodians mistook her spartan room for a vacant one and unloaded a number of stored suitcases and wardrobe bags there.

"You know," Dorothy says to Martin as she discretely breaks off half of another croissant, "Alice could have her own little apartment here. We could make a suite of her and the boys' rooms. It wouldn't be that difficult setting up a kitchen for her, would it?"

Martin leans over the table, looks out the corner of his eye towards Lorna at work in the den. "Let her go," he says quietly. "She wouldn't appreciate anything you did for her anyway."

Dorothy sighs. Perhaps Martin is hurt because Allie prefers to be unemployed rather than go to work for him. He practically had a fit when Dorothy ironed a shirt for the girl before one of her interviews. Well. Well. She loves her husband more than anything, but he *is* getting bossy with age. Maybe he just doesn't feel there's time to talk things out anymore. She doesn't know. *She* was fifty-nine last May and has begun to think maybe all there *is* time for is talking things out.

Into the room comes Alice with a coffee cup. Leftover coconut cream, Dorothy believes, and marvels again at the girl's sudden interest in things caloric. Alice slips the Want Ads out of the papers and sits down to read. Her hair is just washed. The sun lays scissors of shine on its surface.

"You look so pretty!" Dorothy says, a catch in her voice.

Alice looks up, blinks. "How'd your little wingding go?" she asks.

"Wonderful, wonderful," Dorothy answers. "I wish you'd come down. The Nielsen boy came with his parents and he asked about you."

Alice opens and closes her eyes repeatedly, making Dorothy wonder if there is some elaborate code to the movements, something she ought to understand. "I had a headache," Alice says.

Martin rubs his eyes with his fists and laughs. "There were some cute get-ups. Some of the younger gals had on their bikini tops and grass skirts — the whole works." He pauses. "I had no idea that Heberling girl was so — curvaceous."

Alice looks at the ceiling. "I thought you looked nice, Mom," she says to Dorothy, who presided over the party in a mumu and a straw hat purchased from a beach boy in Samoa. She rushes on before her mother, appreciative almost to the point of tears, can say a word:

"I went to a costume party last spring. Warren wanted us to go as Rousseau's 'Sleeping Gypsy.' I think the main thing was he wanted to be a lion. Anyway, I was the gypsy, whole hog, with my hair sprayed black and my skin brown. I wore that striped thing you gave me, Mom." She rolls her eyes. "Warren thought I was *wonderful*. Exotic."

"I'm sure you were," Dorothy says. "You were always striking with a tan, especially when you wore eye make-up. I was wondering if you might — "

"We got to the party, and this couple on the couch was posing as 'The Pieta,' you know, a guy in diapers lying over this woman's lap." Alice sticks out her tongue. "Yuck."

"Oh, my," says Dorothy, warmed by the fact that she and Alice seem to be of one mind, and Alice is talking.

"Well, here *I* was with this proprietal *cat*," Alice says. "I asked myself, 'Is this really any better?' and then I headed straight for the bottle of Ivory Liquid." She laughs, runs her finger down one of the centerpiece's bright blossoms. "Later on, I found the lion in the bathroom kissing a rabbit in tails and a top hat. Mona Lisa," she mumbles. She snaps an orange bloom off a flower head and twirls it between thumb and index finger. "Aaeeh-h-h, what's-up, doc?" she says.

In one breath, Martin and Dorothy begin to object to the destruction, but then the phones are ringing throughout the house, their jangles converging at the dining room. The sucking storm of the vacuum cleaner dies in the den. "You want me to get that, Mrs. Debbins?" calls Lorna.

"Please," Dorothy says, glad of the woman's presence. When Alice decided to live with a black football player during her freshman year, there was no one Dorothy could tell, not even Martin, and then she thought of Lorna. Lorna, herself, had a cousin who had made a disastrous marriage to a black man; Lorna agreed Alice was making a terrible mistake. At Dorothy's request, she wrote Alice a letter to that effect, and Alice hasn't spoken to her since.

"It's for Allie," Lorna calls. Dorothy looks to the girl to see if she will answer or not, but Alice is already on the rise, pushing back from the table in such a rush that Dorothy's coffee sloshes into its saucer. Martin gives Dorothy a look. "Gad, gad," he said, when he finally learned about the black football player. "Next thing you know, she'll bring home a Chinaman."

"Oh, you're kidding!" Alice is saying into the telephone when Dorothy enters the den. Lorna, who sits on the couch, lacklusterly polishing the magazine table, mouths to Dorothy, "I don't know who." A stack of *Architectural Digests* are out of line, and Dorothy straightens them. She wanders over to her desk and riffles through a stack of mail. "Who is it?" she mouths to Alice, but the girl ignores her.

"I've got a job at the Pirate's Store!" Alice announces when she gets off the phone.

"What's the Pirate's Store?" Dorothy says, heart tight, enfisted. Alice's smile is so broad points of white show in her chin, her nose, her cheeks.

"I been there," says Lorna. "It's that import place Mrs. Duffy was telling you about for candles."

"You'd love it, Dorothy," Alice says. "It's got everything."

* * *

This is on Saturday. Alice is to start work on Monday, and, please, no arguments. She goes out that very afternoon, and finds an apartment. Dorothy sits quiet in the car as the smiling girl directs Martin past a dismal string of waterbed shops, tropical fish places, low buildings with concrete block walls painted pale blue, coral, black.

"You can take most anything you want from the house," Dorothy says as Martin turns down a freshly creosoted road.

"Oh, but I'll want to get my own stuff!" Alice says, patting Dorothy on the knee. "Right at the corner, Dad."

"We've got extra everything," Dorothy objects.

"I still have the table and chairs you let Greg and me use."

"Don't remind me!" Dorothy says. Greg was after the football player and before Warren.

"He pines for me, dear, he's skin and bones," Alice says. "It's the gray one, Dad, there."

They pull up in front of a squat, newish building faced with four aluminum windows and a white door aiming at French provincial. Martin clears his throat. "I remember when you and that boob came to visit and when the toast was done, he got himself one of the pieces and left the other in the toaster."

"Cut off his head, the lout!" Alice cries, and bangs a tattoo on the dash. Dorothy recalls, however, that by the end of the visit, in a rare moment of camaraderie, she and Alice ended up in the bathroom, laughing over the noise Greg made when he chewed.

"So," Martin says when they are inside the apartment. The gray linoleum, a moonscape of pocks left by the previous occupant's couches and tables and chairs, makes Dorothy want to cry. "So," Martin says. He raps on the walls with his knuckles, indicating the flimsiness of the plasterboard, "So now you're a working woman."

And, later, to Dorothy, as they are on their way to meet the Hoppers for dinner, "She's just trying to get our goats. Don't you pay any attention to her, Dorothy, no attention at all."

* * *

Dorothy lets a week pass before she goes to the store, but she drives by on several occasions, always finding Alice's red BMW a surprise; perhaps a coincidence, right down to the numbers on the plates? But, no, when she finally does park next to the car, she experiences a little thrill; there is Alice's hooded sweatshirt, and, in the backseat, the six-pack of soda bottles she asked the girl to return several weeks before.

A string of Indian bells rings when she enters the store. In the cabana housing the cash register, two teenaged clerks stop their throwing of courtesy peanuts at one another's mouths, compose their faces, and look to see who has come in.

Dorothy is benumbed by the store's dust and density, the racks of rough shirts from India, the rugs, metal toys, scent of incense and candles. As if she has come into the dark of a movie house after the show has begun, she must stop, one hand on a rack of foreign cookbooks, in order to get her bearings.

She moves past flags into kitchen utensils. Awaiting her are whisks and pastry cloths, buttermelters enamelled navy beneath a fuzz of dust. She looks up and down the aisle for Alice, and there is her *own* face, scattered over a display of mirrors, some of which bear fake cracks, or read, "Mirror, mirror, on the wall . . ." Dorothy looks away in discomfort, opens a small papier mache box and peers inside. Nothing there, of course, nothing.

She heads back towards the cabana and the giggling girls.

"You're her mother!" one of the girls cries when Dorothy asks for Alice. She sputters laughter, her coworker joins in. Dorothy fixes a cold eye on them both, and thinks cruel thought about their tortuous wings of hair and peacock eye shadow. "Try me!" reads a card taped to a bowl on the counter, and, in an effort at *sang-froid*, Dorothy fingers a nut up the side of the dish.

"I'm sorry," the girl says weakly. She escorts Dorothy to the backroom where Alice, up to her ankles in shredded paper, is unloading coffee mugs decorated with plump cats.

"Dorothy!" Alice says, her cheeks reddening. "What happened? Did all your candles burn out?"

"Can't your old mom come and see you?" Dorothy says. She presses her cheek against Alice's, which is cool, and this coolness, mingled with the smell of paper, casts Dorothy back years and years, to naps in the college library, her own cheek resting on the pages of a book.

"What a pretty thing!" Dorothy lifts an enormous egg, creamy and polished as old piano ivories, from a stack of placemats. The small ragged

14

squares chipped from either end remind her of the children's, her own Easters — bright spots before the eyes as she blew-out eggs.

"Ostrich," Alice says happily. "Do you like it? I like it, too!"

"There'd be enough in one of them for my whole family," the counter girl says with a laugh. Dorothy watches Alice turn on the girl, eyes narrowing, the pure blue growing dark; then the eyes flick open, the blue fills with light, light wild and scattered as the crystals in the geode which holds Dorothy's papers on her desk.

"But I bet you missed the wooden fingers and the monster banks!" Alice says.

"What are the wooden fingers?" Dorothy asks.

Alice laughs. She makes the obscene gesture, then pats shocked Dorothy on the arm. "There are rugs, too. I bet you didn't see the rugs and the postcards yet. And the Japanese crackers, you might go for those."

Dorothy smiles. "There's a lot to take in, dear."

"Hey, this is the cave of the Forty Thieves, man!" Alice snaps her fingers. "Don't you remember those pictures where there was so much razzle dazzle and golden rings and lamps that the artist had to forget including all the stuff, so he just made some sort of *shine* there in the background?"

"Who's out there?" a voice calls from a cubicle set against the store's rear wall.

Alice guides Dorothy over to the tiny office where the store manager leans back in his squeaking swivel chair, feet crossed at the ankles and propped on the cluttered desk top. He wears a tiger's eye ring and a paisley tie. On the wall behind him is a poster of the rear end of a horse and, another, of a woman offering whipped-cream and cherry-topped breasts for consumption. Dorothy, embarrassed and offended, looks out a small window between the two. A woman in a red Budweiser cap stops in front of the window and lifts a small red papier mache box, removes the lid and looks inside.

"That's my mirrored spy-hole," the manager says, and winks at Dorothy. "I got regular mirrors all around it. The only guy ever figured it out was trying to take the thing off 'cause he wanted to buy it. Now *that* was funny!"

Dorothy smiles politely. Politely, she buys some candles and a box of chopsticks. She tries, as she walks past the display of mirrors, to determine which mirror is which. To Alice, she whispers, "That man is so awful, honey, I can hardly see how you can bear working for him."

Alice squeezes her eyes shut tight, lifts her shoulders almost as high as her ears. "Mom!" she says, clapping her hands together, "He reminds me exactly of Daddy!"

* * *

Dorothy worries. She loses sleep. In her head, while she gardens, while she listens to a lecture on netsukis she practices entrances to unpredictable conversations: "Well, Alice . . ." "I'm wondering, Alice . . ." "I've noticed, Alice . . ."

15

On the phone, Alice is evasive. She's decorating her apartment, she tells Dorothy, she's bought a cat, she'll invite Dorothy over soon.

Dorothy forwards Alice's few pieces of mail (an alumni bulletin, an invitation to a trunk showing), adding a restrained "Hi — Mom" on the backs of the envelopes. While she is adding Alice's new address to a picture postcard (which she first mistakes for a shot of pink flamingo legs, then recognizes as palm trees in a Forida sunset) she cannot help but notice the sender is a very nice boy Alice dated in high school. "Dear Alley Cat," the card begins. Several of the next lines are indecipherable, a child's imitation of cursive writing, but the jist of the card is that the fellow is drunk, on a honeymoon, and will love Alice for ever and ever. The postscript is both obscene and insulting. Reading it makes Dorothy's cheeks grow quite warm, just below her eyes, as if someone has rubbed a hot soup spoon back and forth on her skin. She puts the card in the trash, but that evening, while Martin is at a board meeting, she retrieves it. A little orange concentrate has dripped on the ink. The address has spread in furry blue flowers. Dorothy sticks her finger in the juice can and drips a bit more of the liquid along the postscript until all that is left on the card is a declaration of love. She sticks the card in an envelope, the envelope in her purse, the purse in the car, and, herself following, drives to the store.

* * *

Alice is in the office, looking out the two-way mirror; respectfully, as if she has come upon a birder in a blind, Dorothy maintains her silence, stays out in the backroom, unannounced.

Beyond the mirrored window glass, a woman about Dorothy's age stops, picks up a glass egg shot with candylike swirls. The woman polishes the egg on her sweater sleeve, looks around, slips the egg into her pocket. Alice does not stir.

"Alice!" Dorothy wants to cry out; instead she backs away from the door, goes out into the shop. Absently, she straightens a row of tea boxes, lining up their robins on cherry boughs, their puffy white clouds in skies of blue. She wanders past a pile of wicker chests, looks at the glass eggs. A blurred voice and knocking comes from behind the mirror-display wall, then Alice is sticking her head out the backroom door. "Hey!" she says, startling Dorothy with her heavily made-up face: glossy lips, eyes powdered blue, lined, lashes beaded with black. "Come on!" she cries, then retracts her head, disappears into the backroom.

"Alice!" Dorothy calls, and hurries after. "Alice!"

She takes a step backward, hands to her mouth.

The girl beams. Her hands rest on her lower belly, which bulges ominously beneath a skirt Dorothy seems to recall from the girl's high school days. "Ta-ta!" Alice says, and lifts the skirt to reveal the stuffed top of her pantyhose. "For you," Alice says, slipping the ostrich egg from the stocking, handing it to Dorothy.

"Allie," Dorothy says, and shakes her head. "Well, thank you, you nut. It really is a beautiful — "

"Listen, I've got to get some things done before I close up," Alice says. She starts Dorothy towards the back door, giving her such insistent pushes on the back that Dorothy tries to catch a look over her shoulder at the girl's face.

"I've got a date with Jim," Alice says.

"Oh!" Dorothy fumbles in her purse for the envelope containing the postcard, presses it into Alice's hand. "Who's Jim?" she asks.

"You know, silly; the manager! And here!" Alice swoops down on a tea set sitting on a pushcart near the door and hands it to Dorothy. "This is for you, too," she says, before giving Dorothy a final shove into the night.

Dorothy starts towards the front of the building. "See you later, alligator," Alice calls after her, and Dorothy automatically picks up the response, a part of Alice's childhood bedtime business: "After a while, crocodile." She turns, smiling, but the door is already closed.

* * *

"She's a kook," Martin says, voice narrowed by the tilt of his chin as he shaves his Adam's apple. He lowers the chin, rinses the razor. "I could have told you that a *long* time ago," he adds, almost happily, as if the duration of such knowledge soothed him and should soothe Dorothy, too.

But Dorothy is miserable. She takes no pleasure in the rust and yellow chrysanthemums blooming in the brick garden beds, or the sugar maple leaves starring the still green lawn. She skips her docent training, leaves bridge club early, going home to think of Alice, wishing the girl's life were something she could hold, turn over in her hands.

Lorna listens. She says, ticking her right index finger against the fingers of her left hand: "She's got a job, she's dressing up, she's dating, she gives you presents; sounds to me like you should be happy, Mrs. Debbins!"

"Well," says Dorothy, realizing she has not told Lorna something about proportion — the width of the eye-liner, the greasiness of the manager.

She calls the boys. "Mom," says the younger, in what she now knows as his professional drawl, "you're getting all worked up over nothing. She's just testing her wings. Anyway," he laughs, "her taste in men always did leave something to be desired. She's always been a kook, if you ask me."

Dorothy goes back to the store and peers in the window. There is Alice, moving through the store, snipping dead leaves from the plants, unloading a box of candles. Dorothy recognizes that custodial calm, remembers moving through her own house when it was on The Heritage Tour, and how she took delight in a little show of intimacy (a stop for a cigarette and a match from a box on a high shelf).

She leaves before the girl can see her, although she feels as if she could stay and stay — as if she has the privilege of seeing, awake, a playback of one of her own dreams.

* * *

17

"Come on over!" Alice says on the phone, and when Dorothy pulls up, Alice is waiting at her apartment window, face theatrically clear; she is a Kabuki, eyes rimmed, plump face white, a patch of red on each cheek. She waves to Dorothy, then disappears, curtain falling back in place.

"Come in, come in!" she cries when Dorothy knocks. She throws the door open so wide the knob hits the wall with a crack. "I'm going to make us tea!" she says, and pulls Dorothy's coat down off her shoulders. She rushes over to one of three wicker throne chairs and drops onto its cushioned seat. She props her feet on a foot high stack of raffia placemats. "I have mints, too," she says, and takes a deep breath. "I have everything."

Dorothy stares. Her high heels are deep in oriental rugs — two? three? The fringe at either end is tangled and knotted. Along the walls are piles of woks, folded flags, brass ashtrays, boxes of chopsticks, boxes of imported teas, a hill of tiny brooms. In the gloom of the bedroom, Dorothy spies the pure white insoles of an entire laundry basket of "coolie slippers."

"When did you — do all this, honey?" she asks finally.

"Little by little," Alice says, looking around the room with obvious satisfaction. She sticks out her lower lip, pulls it in. "I like it," she says. "I like what I do. My boss says the plants never looked better, but they're going to get rid of them because of shipping problems. Except cacti. We'll still have cacti." She rests her cheek upon the chair arm. "Woo!" she says, then hops up. "Would you like some tea? It's Oolong. Do you like Ooooooooolong?"

"That's fine. The table looks lovely, dear, such pretty flowers." She follows Alice over to the sink-stove affair that is the kitchen. "Maybe you'd like to move back to the house for a while, have you thought of that?"

Alice giggles, and not at all madly, but as she did when she was a child, hair cut in a jagged "pixie," body shivering while she waited for Dorothy to dry her off after a swim. She pauses, thumps her chest with a fist. "This is my house now, Dorothy," she says, her voice that of a very young child imitating a grown-up. "I have to live in my house."

Dorothy puts a hand on Alice's shoulder, as much to steady herself as to gauge the girl's internal weather. The water thunders into the tea kettle.

Alice takes a wooden match from a box, turns, alert as a hunter. "Shh!' she says, her voice so angry Dorothy draws her own hand off the girl's shoulder; then, just as abruptly, Alice is apologizing in a hostess's honeyed voice: "Sorry, Dorothy, you were saying?"

"Nothing. I wasn't saying anything," Dorothy answers, while, like one of the agates her father polished in the tumbling box he bought for his retirement, tumbling, over and over, abraded until it is smooth and shining and revealed, her brain rolls. She pulls out a chair for herself at the card table and sits. Alice strikes the match in her hand, spreads its blue through the hiss of burning gas.

On the table there is a small cardboard box of wooden tops. The tops are painted to look like apples. Dorothy picks one up by the stem, spins it, and in the spinning, the apple becomes a striped ball.

"Graham crackers with butter would be good, don't you think?" Alice asks.

"Yes, fine."

The tea kettle's whistle begins. "It's time!" Alice cries, and pours the boiling water into the tea pot. She sits down at the table, takes Dorothy's hands in hers, squeezes them as a person might squeeze her own hands while worried. "I've always loved your hands," she says absently. "I used to put on the rings you weren't wearing and stand in front of the mirror. Just to look at my hand and pretend it was yours." She runs her finger along one of her mother's ropey veins, then rests her face on the hand.

Dorothy strokes the top of the girl's head, amazed by how the long blond hair has grown coarse over the years and no longer slips through her fingers, watery fine.

Alice jumps up for the pot. "Company first," she says. She fills a cup — doll-sized, pink — with the smoky tea, and smiles, and drinks.

WILL

A cool, slim Diahann Carroll is on the talk show. She says to Totie Fields — who makes a living joking about her supply of adipose, yet dresses in the kind of wafting chiffons favored by Liz Taylor — Diahann Carroll says, "Totie, my own favorite thing to eat is a hot fudge sundae."

Whether they are on together, separately, whether they are different people all together, I know the talk is going to come around to food eventually: How does Diahann stay so thin? Banter between the host and Totie. Cookies. Ding-dongs. Baked beans.

The host and Totie and the audience gasp and lean forward, tell us more, when Diahann mentions the hot fudge sundae. Really? Hot fudge?

She smiles, lets us in on her secret: she has not eaten one in fifteen years.

Ah! The audience sits back, relieved, on their KrumKakes, Cheetos, Big Macs and raised doughnuts. She has not eaten one in fifteen years.

I unbutton my blouse and begin to nurse the baby. Fifteen years! I think, and am filled with wonder. Fifteen years of restraint. It takes all I've got to keep from calling my old boyfriends — who might not dig the stretch marks on my belly — and suggesting suggestions. Who can worry about hot fudge, hey?

"Don't you think," the host suggests, "that it was excessive, Diahann, your spending three days preparing for The Academy Awards?"

Usually, I'd agree. I never can talk, at least not really, to a woman with a manicure; I just end up staring at her nails, trying to figure out if she got the polish right, and if she did, I think she's an idiot, anyway, wasting her time like that. But today, no, I don't like the way that host is smiling, the edges of his mouth turned up like the rim on a saucer. I think, Fuck off, fuck face, while he teases Diahann about facials and all, and a sudden burst of audience laughter sends the camera on a quick and wobbly trip to the dark sides of the stage, the end of the world, where a young man is stepping into the light, two American-dream sundaes in his hands, the mountains of whipped cream beginning to topple as they are carried toward Diahann and Totie.

This is a scream, thinks the host. His boyish cheeks bunch under his eyes. Everything on his show is a scream, or else it is meaningful. "Wake up!" I shout to myself when I feel a little moved by his victims, reunions, tributes. On his show, even Jerry Lewis is meaningful. Jerry Lewis's eyes juggle with appreciation for his meaningfulness, his tender side not shrieking imitation opera or talking baby talk for the moment.

Someone has forgotten the spoons. Totie Fields tries to take a gobble at the sundae, who cares? Diahann Carroll tries to stop her. Totie! This results in Totie's fat face being smeared with the whipped cream. Diahann Carroll laughs and sits back, two globs of whipped cream clinging to her slim black fingers, but she does not lick the sweetness off, no. She holds up her hand and waits. Someone from offstage brings her a tissue and she wipes the whipped cream away as though it were a lotion which had something to do with her being so svelte and lovely.

I sit forward in my chair, making the baby uncomfortable. He snuffles and snorts. He gives me a good bite which brings tears to my eyes. "All over for you, soon, buddy boy," I say, and stick him in his infant pouch. In spite of what the ads say, his weight *does* pull at the straps around my neck, hard; but he likes the thing, he's happy hanging on my front, and it's better than the crying. He's been a crier since the day he was born.

We walk into the kitchen, which looks pretty bad, but I'm just going to think dishes, now, I'm not going to think about anything else. If I get the dishes done before Jerry gets home, that will be enough after the laundromat and the diaper pail and everything else you don't want to hear about. It's not easy washing dishes with a baby dangling from your front, it's like I'm pregnant; I have to stand sideways to the sink. Every once in a while I kiss the top of the baby's head, shoulders. It's a comfort. "Lanugo," I whisper. I don't know whether it sounds nice or obscene, but I mean it to sound nice.

Do you know, I'm always here, looking out the window over the sink? I'm here at six every morning, looking out while I fill the coffee pot; at noon while I wash up the lunch dishes, before dinner, during, after — noon, afternoon, evening. I must be here all the time since I never miss Jerry pulling into the drive. I'm always at the door before he's out of the truck.

I knock on the window while he's getting something out of the back end, and without even raising his head to see who it is — it has to be me, who else could it be? — he lifts his arm for a hello.

I think, while I'm waiting at the door — because you can't look too eager — I think, who was the worst? The host, I decide, because he encouraged them. He was the worst, then Diahann, then Totie. No, Totie was worse than Diahann because she was making money off being fat. Or was Diahann worse, being so cool, so absolutely under control?

"Who's worse?" I ask Jerry, who smells like motor oil and leaves finger prints on my clothes, on the baby, but I don't mind. "I'll tell you," I say, and follow him into the shower.

I don't know then that, while getting a face lift, Totie Fields will develop phlebitis and lose her leg, and, shortly after, all her fat, and then, shortly after that, from complications, her life; or that Diahann Carroll's movie career will come to a stand still and she will appear only in glossy magazines discussing things like the way she contours, doesn't contour her face; or that the host will lose his show; or that I will call some of my old boyfriends — who will not seem to mind the stretch marks on my belly (which fade to almost nothing, after all) — and that I will suggest some suggestions.

21

CRIME IN ITALY

On their way to the car, Zach chanted:
>This is the rat
>That killed the cat
>that ate the —

He stopped, shook his pale blond head.

"The *cat* that killed the *rat*," she told him, though sympathetic to the nature of his error. "The rat that ate the malt."

And who was *she*? She was the mother, Sandy, nee Farmer, turned Haller, now Bozocowski, who herded Zach and the other kids into the car, where, immediately, they began to complain about the upholstery.

"It's burning!" cried Zach. Nicole, scrambling across the floor mat on her knees, extended a cautious finger to a seat belt buckle. "Ow! No belts!" she said, imitating her big brother's frown.

"Piffle." Sandy liked that: piffle. Such a perfect dismissal; but when she bent into the Chevy with Ginny's infant seat, the dust and heat rose to her in a sickening wave: the children were right. She backed into the blazing day, damped the sweat from her upperlip with her finger. "Well, come on, we've got to get going, anyway," she said.

Nicole pointed over Sandy's shoulder. "Here come John."

"Don't park the car there, honey, we're just leaving," Sandy called in the direction of a slate-blue Monte Carlo. Her husband. The doctor. He rose from the car like an enormous bubble, a cloud. Sometimes — pale-skinned, dark-haired, huge — he reminded her of one of the sad and funny pandas in the children's books, but he could change, slide back and forth like pictures she'd had in her intro psych book: the old hag becomes the elegant lady with her face turned away from the viewer becomes the old hag again. He left the car where it was.

"How do I look?" Sandy asked. She was pretty, anyway (dark cap of curls, ivory skin) — but today she'd taken special pains —

"Where are you going?" He hiked his trousers with a frown.

"I told you, honey, lunch with Amy Trouder."

"What about my lunch?"

"I do feel sorry for you, hon, but I'll get over it." She laughed, tickled his waist, just hoping she could get away without trouble. Last Wednesday, he'd told her — words squeezing around the edges of the gun stuck in his mouth — he'd told her he would kill himself if she and the kids went to visit her mother out in Montana. Maybe it was all dramatics, but Sandy threw up just the same. Her mom was furious about the divorce, the marriage to John: she didn't even *want* Sandy to come to Montana.

John peered into the car at the sweating, wide-eyed children. Across his broad back, his suit jacket had creased in a great, anxious X. He spun around, grabbing Sandy's face, hard, just below the cheekbones. "You'll be seeing Mick," he said accusingly.

"Just when I drop them off. You're the one who said he couldn't come here, babe."

"Babe," he snorted. He kicked at a rag coiled on the drive, and it flipped — damp side up — onto the bleached and splintered yew near the garage. The front door he let slam after himself.

Sandy smiled at the kids as if nothing had happened, then ran through a brief but nerve-wracking filmstrip of herself moving John's car, her car, John's car. No thank you. "Come on, guys," she said, scooping up the baby and safety seat, feeling mightily wild, energized by action in the face of despair. "We're taking the Monte Carlo."

She had a right to it, she thought, as she backed out the drive. The damn thing wasn't paid for; *it* was the reason she'd had to go back to work. A nice surprise for a woman with three kids all under six, especially from a man who'd been all gungho about her going back to school before she married him. "If you were my wife," he'd said, his hands smoothing her cheekbones. If you were my wife.

She started the kids off:

> Over in the meadow in the sand in the sun
> Lived an old mother turtle and her little turtle one.
> DIG! said the mother —

They passed through verses in which mother animals and their babies dug and swam and wooed and gnawed and buzzed and cawed and jumped and baahed and quacked and beaved, yes, beaved, before the Monte Carlo pulled into the parking lot where Mick was waiting.

Mick had bought a pickup after the divorce. Red, with fat tires and four-wheel drive. He was parked out of the sun in this vehicle, snoozed-back in the seat, a cowboy hat tilted over his eyes.

"Ha!" Sandy said aloud, but she kept her name-calling out of the kiddies' hearing: Mr. Dude! Mr. Fatty! El Studo! Boozer. Pothead. Creep. She was glad she was driving John's car, the machine as solid as an embrace. She parked at the foot of the drive-in's golden arches, forgetting in her nervousness that it was necessary to shift into neutral; when she took her foot off the brake, the car leapt forward, made a noise loud and ugly as something escaping from the body — and died.

"Clunk!" shouted Zach. In the back seat, Nicole shrieked, the baby babbled an alarm. Sandy pretended nothing had happened; but she *knew* Mick was watching. He'd make some remark. He'd sit there in that damn truck as if he didn't see them coming, and then he'd make some remark. "Dr. B's car giving you trouble, lady?" Something like that. He and John had worked together in the mills before John went off to some special school for chiropractors. They'd been friends. Which was not Sandy's fault. Why anyone would want to be friends with either of them was beyond her, ha, ha.

She stretched her neck back over the seat. Nicole was just finishing tucking her dress into her lace panties. "Nicole," Sandy said, and pointed a finger at the offending underwear. The child looked up, startled. Sandy felt herself transformed into Cinderella's stepmother, mouth stitching itself into a dangerous elegant purse. Such skills, such disguises! she thought; here she really meant to be Cinderella, and look what happened!

Her face slid across the surface of the rearview mirror. She retrieved a blip of mascara which had abandoned her lashes. Was Mick watching? She'd have to make it clear all this shadow and shine wasn't for him. "Criminitly," she said, slowly, deliberately, as she let the kids out of the car. Judy Trew had told her the exclamation wasn't nonsense, it really came from somewhere: "Italians, you know, the Mafia? *Crime in Italy.*" Happy for the explanation, Sandy added the word to her supply. Crime in Italy. Once, at some point in the mess of their mutual histories, Mick and John had sat in Sandy and Mick's living room — stoned to de bone, as Mick liked to say: two huge men, roaring, shaking the floor with their feet. John stumbled into the kitchen "I'm going to make you an offer you can't refuse," he said to Sandy. While she was laughing, he kissed her, just a little kiss, a joke kiss, but that and the imitation Marlon Brando were what did it. "The Baby Machine fell off her chair!" he'd shouted into Mick; Mick had said okay, but stayed in with Johnny Carson. After Mick, John had seemed like a miracle.

Now, across the parking lot, behind the pickup's tinted glass, Mick lifted his head, the hat rising, the face beneath seeming a pale something falling from the brim. Sandy suspected her dress was hitched-up on one side, where the baby rode her hip, but her other hand held the safety seat; she could do nothing to improve the situation.

"Daddy!" Zach shouted and ran on ahead, careless of cars. "Zach!" Sandy cried, but he was already swinging from the doorhandle. Mick stuck a big, furry arm out the window, mussed Zach's hair. "How you doing, kid?" he said. He waved down to Nicole, wiggled a remote finger at eight-month old Ginny; since the divorce three months before, he acted as if there were some question about Ginny, though she was blond and blue-eyed as the other two, all three of them clones of Mick's baby pictures. "Got your party clothes on, huh, Nicole?" he said.

Clearly, he was going to pretend Sandy wasn't there. But he didn't fool her. She'd seen his truck glide by the house. She suspected he'd gone on nights at the mill so he could mosey past the house while John was at the clinic. "I see you more now than when we were married," she might have said, but she didn't, partly because on Tuesday she had been looking out the kitchen window at the same moment he had been looking in: both of them so surprised they hadn't even looked away.

She shifted the baby on her hip. "You going to open the door, Mick?" she asked, "Or do you just plan on sitting there all day?"

He tilted his head towards some invisible partner. As if vastly amused, he stabbed his index finger into his palm: get her. On his neck stood bright blond stubble, longer than if he'd just skipped a shave or two. She could just imagine one of those sleazes he'd been hanging out with: "Oh, Mick, you'd look so *good* with a beard!"

"Let's go!" Zach shouted. "I want to go!"

"I'm talking to your father," said Sandy. Mick snorted. A long pheasant feather waved above his hat; Sandy found it corny, depressing. He was balding under that hat. Still a surprise, the ridged scalp. They'd gone together since she was fifteen, him with his hair standing straight up, thick and blond as the bristles on her Grandma's dresser brush. She wanted to tell him about John and that gun business, to make it sound funny or something.

"So, how're you doing, Sandy?" he asked. She nodded. The baby put her moist hand on the door lock, father and mother watching her struggle to move it. "That a girl!" Mick said. "Where you off to, Sandy? Got a doctor appointment?"

"Hh! I might be going somewhere else!"

"Forget I asked. Ex*cuse* me."

She stared off across the lot, as if the trees and the hot road and the gas station converted into something called a Pop Shoppe were waiting for her, waiting for Sandy. She said, "I'm meeting Amy Trouder for lunch. She's living in Gary now."

"That girl from the University? Sure. Cute chick. She married?"

Sandy shook her head, not just to answer Mick's question, but to get it out of her head. When she had told Amy she was leaving college to marry Mick, Amy's blue eyes opened so wide a small bird could have flown in and taken-up residence in her head. "*Him*? Him?" Amy had said. "When you could take your pick of any guy, him?" Sandy was still pleased she had just smiled, not made up words where there weren't any.

Now, to Mick, she said, "Amy and I started school at the same time; now she's teaching people how to be nurses. What have I got to show?"

"You married the doctor, Sandy, that's what all the nurses want." He grinned and tapped his ring against the steering wheel: Here comes the bride. She stuck her tongue out at him, but couldn't help laughing. Even the idea of John as a doctor struck her funny. "Bone cracker," her mom had said, "just a damn bone cracker."

"I was going to ask if you wanted something to eat," Mick said. Out the window came his hand, stroked the baby's head. The stroke moved through the child to Sandy's breast, chilling, exciting, as if Mick were someone else, not the man who'd told her she should consider implants. Implants! So now she couldn't pass a mirror without checking the drape of her shirt. "I guess I have to go," she said.

Mick shifted in the enormous space-absorbing way he and John shared — a movement which sometimes left her feeling that she was part of a great supply of warmth and solidity, and, alternately, that no comfort remained in the world for her, they'd used it all up. At the moment, seeing his little smile, she felt the latter. "Now you understand I can't take Ginny, right?" he said.

She dangled the safety seat from a finger — heavy, heavy — and waited, trying hard to remember what they'd told her in assertiveness training, but it was no good. She didn't want to start crying. She figured she could keep from crying, but beyond that — "Mick, you've got to take her!" she pleaded. "This is the first time in years I've had the chance."

He held his hands up in front of himself, victim of a robbery. "We're going to Ray and Connie's place, there's going to be a picnic or something. No provisions for a baby."

No provisions! He'd sure practiced that line. Connie and Ray's! A filthy house, crumbs of dope and toast on every flat surface. The last time she'd been there with Mick, she'd looked up to see a totally naked woman dancing on the roof; a cat had been eating an opossum on the kitchen floor.

"You're not taking them there," she said firmly.

"Well, I am."

Even with the baby in one arm, she was able to swing the infant seat, bring it up to the door with a crack. *Then* he was out of the truck fast enough, with Nicole crying, Zach dancing between the truck and the neighboring car — whose air-conditioned inhabitants looked away under Sandy's glare.

"Damn you!" Mick said. His face was very pink. "There better not be no scratch, lady."

"Oh, you and your mill talk! There's no scratch," she said, though she wouldn't have cared if there were. She felt suddenly hot and drowsy, as if she'd been lying out in the sun for hours and just stood up. Distantly, the underside of her chin brushing the baby's fluffy hair, she watched Mick smooth his thick fingers over places she knew she hadn't even come close to. "See, there's no scratch," she said, and held the safety seat out to him.

He tossed the seat into the pickup, yanked the baby from her arms. "Bitch," he said, which made Zach grin.

"That's a nice way to talk in front of the kids." She tipped close to him, hissed, "You better stay straight till you get these kids back to me, you understand?" She crouched to the children for goodbyes; and, feeling cool, shakily defiant, started towards the car. Her hips she let sway in exaggeration, not so he'd think she was sexy, really, just to remain visible, not fade away.

He had his own response: lay on the horn, peel out of the lot, the kids bouncing on the pickup's seat like loose packages.

She was not going to let this ruin her day, thank you, no, no, no, no. She lay her forehead against the hot steering wheel for a brief moment, taking strength from that crescent of pressure. Then she started the car, Paul Harvey was giving a rundown of ancient marriages; she punched her way to WLS, where some sweet male sang about changes of heart, and told her that if she ever had one, he'd be waiting for her still. She thought of the red lines shown in every science book they'd ever given her at school — lines crisp and jagged as rickrack, coming off the friendly radio tower which carried her this song. She wanted to cry, and not because the song made her think of John or Mick, no, the song made her think of a delicious someone else who would treasure her as a lover ought to treasure the beloved. A tootling sound ran through the music. Like the notes from the black plastic instrument they all kept in their desks during fifth grade. The Tonette, the only instrument she had ever learned to play; though she'd envied the girls who learned to bow over thrumming guitars, waterfalls of hair concealing their art, the Tonette was as far as she'd gotten. For years, she'd bumped into that thing while looking for something else. In her mom's junk drawer? The mitten basket? She could imagine it just about anywhere now: in some box dragged off to Montana; in the carton of notes and photo albums and cheerleading stuff Mick had taken to the dump after she and the kids moved out; sprouting wings and flying off over the dark mills of Gary into cooler, clearer skies.

* * *

The restaurant was dark, multileveled, decorated in wood and enormous coins, big as cartwheels, some of them: The Gold Piece. A man with a black patch over one eye greeted them at the door. She wondered if he considered her attractive, or if he just noticed Amy with her waist-length blond hair. He was thin. Sandy herself was thin. She liked thin. Why did she marry fat? Huge? Enormous? "Glad to get out of that heat?" the man said. Both Sandy and Amy sighed and pronounced emphatic yes's. His eye patch was sad. And brave. Sandy's heart beat fast with happiness and sympathy. If this man were her husband, she wouldn't care about his eye; she'd have him take the patch off before they made love so nothing would stand between them.

At a table looking out over the lower level of the restaurant, she and Amy traded sips of their daiquiris (strawberry, banana) and shivered. "This is really a nice place," said Sandy when the waitress came back with the menus. She looked up to smile at the young woman, found large breasts beneath emblazoned black cotton: GOLD PIECE. Then there was the face, and above that, the lights, the ceiling with enormous dollar bills disappearing beneath wooden beams. A crescent of George Washington's weak chin, left forlorn.

"You notice the boobs on the waitresses here?" Amy whispered after the young woman left. Sandy, still blushing, took a look around the room, nodded, giggled; she was glad Amy made large breasts sound like something funny.

"What's good to eat?"

"I like Fort Knox," Amy said. "It's really a chef salad. Everything here's got a name connected with money or something.'

Sandy decided on a perch platter. "Big Jim Fish," the waitress said, her smile containing a touch of reprimand for Sandy's not using the correct name. Amy began a tale of nursing school policy. She worked her hands beneath her long hair, and arranged it behind her shoulders as she talked; the gesture reminded Sandy of her Grandma Farmer maneuvering a pie dough into a pan.

"And *Del* is trying to get in with Stuart. Piss me off!" Amy finished. Sandy thought she remembered a Del slightly, a smart girl with thick eyebrows, but who was Stuart? Who were Mobley and Christy?

"I need a break," said Amy, "a little time without any pressures, not stuffing this school crap in my head all day long." She dipped low over her drink, not bothering to lift the glass from the table, and sipped from the swizzle straw.

Sandy considered a thoughtful response. She smoothed her finger along the white edge of a glossy placard on the table. TRY OUR DAIQUIRIS: SIX FABULOUS FLAVORS. The card's photo showed much larger containers of much brighter liquids than those before Amy and Sandy. Sandy turned the card. Both sides were the same.

"I wanna feel like I don't have to accomplish anything," Amy said. "It's been ages since I felt really good about just being me, you know?"

Sandy brightened, not because she wanted Amy to be unhappy, but here was a chance to talk about her problems with John. "When was the last time you did feel really good, Amy?" she asked; but was immediately embarrassed by how awful the question sounded, as if she were the group-leader in assert-iveness class or something. Amy, however, looked pleased; apparently Sandy had asked the right question. Wasn't that just the way?

"Hmm," Amy said luxuriously. She closed her eyes, opened them very suddenly. "It's been a *loooooong* time, Sandy," she said. She grinned, she shook her head, smiled at the businessmen at the next table. The men smiled back. "Just singing the blues!" she called over to them; the men laughed a little, nodded.

Sandy shifted in her chair, turning away from that cluster of faces. You weren't supposed to expect too much from friends, Sandy knew that, but still, she felt cheated. She felt an urge to stick a pin into such nonsense. "How'd you get unhappy, Amy?" she asked. Amy faced Sandy again, but Sandy didn't wait for an answer. "Maybe it'll be a long time before you feel happy again," she said.

Amy looked about the room, eyes narrow as a cat's — as if pleasant things were mysteriously sprouting out of the walls for her. She said: "I think things are going to be better real soon, Sandy."

Just like that. Sandy shrugged. "You still seeing Don?" she asked.

"Yeah." Amy shook her head, rapped her long nails on the table. "Don's got marriage on the brain."

Delight and envy quickened in Sandy. Amy became new. A nurse. A bride. A wife. A sister of sorts. "So marry him!" she said, but the words sobered her. "Well, maybe marry him." She sunk her chin into a cup formed of palms and fingers, wiggled her jaw back and forth. "*Some* animals can make it for life, I hear. Cardinals? And isn't it swans? Swans too?" She giggled.

"People are the only ones who get *married*, silly," said Amy. "That counts for something."

With words rising like bubbles, dislodging a clot of teariness, Sandy said, "They're the ones who need to." She grinned at Amy, coughed.

"Are you being real, or just goofy?" Amy asked.

Sandy pulled her face long, trying to retrieve the tears. "Just goofy. I gotta use the restroom, excuse me — " She rose from her chair, awkward, bumped into the balcony rail. The table of businessmen politely reeled-in their smiles and looked away. On the glimmering edge of her vision — all that dark punctuated with discs of gold and silver — she had a sense of the man with the patch watching her descend the stairs. She headed towards the back of the restaurant. Another short flight of stairs rose up on the right and she took it.

The room at the top was dark, and in that dark, chilled shapes sped, fell through space with electronic pings, were replaced by squared letters. She felt as if she's stepped inside someone's brain, where possible creatures waited in the dark to do you harm. At the sound of a voice, she jumped:

"If you're looking for the cigarette machine, it's right through the hall here, next to the restrooms." The man with the patch, a hand on each banister, his torso relaxing forward like he might be about to do some brief exercise. "Sorry if I scared you."

She shook her head, thanked him.

The restroom's paper towels smelled good in an odd way, like a woods. Wood. Wood was what it came from. She sniffed appreciatively. It was important to have a good time! Babysitters were damned expensive and hard to find. The last one she used was only a sixth-grader. Being conversational, in the car-ride home, Sandy had asked, "How're things going?" The girl had said, "My parents are getting divorced." It was not easy at such times to sit on your comforter instincts, but Sandy sensed the girl's answer was no plea for sympathy, it was simply what rode the top of her brain. Some pair they were, the two of them sniffling their way up to the father's new apartment! A slender young man opened the door, but when Sandy put out her hand, the girl cried, "*He's* not my dad," and ran from the room. Father — pale, distraught, a dishtowel in hand — stepped from the kitchen; he looked at Sandy, down the hall from his daughter. Sandy felt responsible for everybody's misery.

Now she set her purse on the restroom sink to see if she had any lipstick; she didn't. What she did have: diaper pins; a few restaurant packs of saltines, crackers a fine dust; Zach's Mickey Mouse Watch minus one hand; an advertising pen in which a tiny semi, captured in clear liquid, drove towards the point when the pen was in use. She pinched her cheeks as Scarlett had done in *Gone With the Wind.* Once, during that year she went away to college, a boy told Sandy she looked like Vivian Leigh. Once, in the eighth grade, Sandy herself kissed a girl, a real kiss, with tongue and all, just to show this girl how it was done. The shock was, it didn't feel any different. Soft and nice and warm. But when the girl begged Sandy to do it again, Sandy was firm in her refusal. Even now, when she knew such things were normal as canned corn, she couldn't get interested in women in that way. For a time, she'd wondered if maybe Mick had a little of that in him, he was so damned uninterested in sex; but then she married John and found out he was the same way after the first month. Men.

* * *

29

Amy, up on the balcony, was pointing at the table, indicating she'd bought them each another drink; although Sandy's first was still two-thirds full, she laughed, she was glad Amy had done it.

"Don't you think that guy with the patch is good-looking?" she whispered as she scooted her chair up to the table.

A slow smile spread across Amy's face. "I think that if he took off — " Amy peered over the balcony, setting Sandy grinning. What would Amy say? His patch? Took off his shirt? All his clothes? But Amy shifted her eyes, indicating Sandy, too, should look. Sandy was already turning at the sound of the voice.

"I don't need a table!" Below, the pallor of John's baldness rose out of his dark hair, the dark room, like the back of a turtle.

"It's John!" Sandy said. Her first impulse was to hide her drinks, but that was too silly, too impossible to carry out. She stood up, fast. If he were looking for her, it wouldn't do for him to think she was hiding. She put herself in plain view, stepping out from behind the table, while up the stairs he came — white shirt, dark pants — everyone turning to look.

"What are you doing here, John?"

His face churned. He lay his hand on top of his head, like a cap. "The children, the babies," he said, voice cranking up like a hand organ. "Your babies are home without any food! Your children are at home, crying!"

The other customers had stopped eating. Down by the bar, the waitresses clustered together; in the dark, the gold letters on their shirts shifted and glowed like embers in a fire. "The children are with Mick, John," she began.

"The children are crying for you!"

She dug in her purse for her wallet. Amy stared warily at John, as if she feared he might go off at any moment. She said: "We met once — "

"Is there a problem here, folks?" The man with the eye patch said.

"She's my wife, you fool!" shouted John. Sandy shoved some bills toward Amy. At her elbow, John was beginning to snuffle and snort, face wet with tears. In spite of herself, in spite of everything, she felt sorry for him.

"That's too much money," said Amy, "really, Sandy."

Sandy held up a hand. "I'll call you," she said.

Down the stairs, past the islands of diners, through the hall, out the door, she preceded John into the day. She was faster than he was. He was big. Her husband. She took his trembling hand. The weight of it came to her separate from him, like the cow tongue she sometimes bought because it made good, cheap sandwiches. Pale and black. Bristled. The children always shrieked over it, then came close to look.

"Here," she said, and leaned him against the building.

Out in the street, her Chevy was double-parked, still running, just where he'd left it. Other cars came up from behind, paused for a moment, then realized no one was inside, and passed.

The sky had changed to a gray watered-satin. Out at Ray and Connie's, Mick and the kids would be having a good time. Mick would trick some responsible girl into watching the baby, she supposed. They'd all get sunburned.

They'd all be crabbing by the time she drove to MacDonald's to pick them up. Maybe she'd sit in the truck for a while. Not too long, but long enough for him to consider the possibility of her. If she went slow, he'd think it was his own idea, letting her come back. He'd have to let her come back, just like she'd have to let herself go back. It wouldn't be progress, there was no denying that, but the kids would have their dad, and she would still be Sandy. Who she was when she met him. Sandy Farmer. It probably wasn't even John's fault he didn't know who she really was; he'd met her when she was somebody else.

She patted him absently on the arm, looked back in the restaurant window. The man with the patch stood at the bar. He gave her a look as if to ask, "Are you okay?" She nodded.

He shook his head and leaned an elbow on the bar. Tired, sorry. She supposed having just one eye was exhausting.

Office workers, business people, shoppers who'd stopped for lunch, she felt their stares. They looked at the man with the patch, then back at her, as if they might understand more by following that gaze.

She didn't care. Let them look. They weren't going to understand a thing. She pressed her mouth to the glass in a kiss, then backed away, eyes closed, and fished for the keys.

IN SPRING

On all fours and on top of the dresser, Carol Cameron backed out her bedroom window. One pale, well-oiled leg stretched for the flat roof below, found it, and the rest of her followed. She looked about herself, into the fat leaves of the oak trees. She snapped her swimsuit bottom into place.

"It's great out here, Kit."

"Kit" leaned out the window. "Isn't that tar hot?"

In a show of pleasure, Carol turned her face up to the sun, closed her eyes, reached high into the air with fingers and arms. When she opened her eyes again, Kit stood next to her: two pretty young women, winter-white, on a roof. A big roof. A roof which extended over the home's entire sunporch. A roof which once inspired Carol to four-square, and a standing broad jump that landed her in the yews below.

Kit inspected a knee ruffled white by a shake. "You're sure this is safe?" she asked.

"Sure, sure." Mention of Carol's mother embarrassed everyone, even Kit, so Carol said only, "We do have to keep quiet, though."

There. Like that. Kit looked down. She said, "Right."

The girls walked to the roof's edge and looked down. It was not far. Below, Carol's father hastily painted a wrought iron love seat. He plunged the brush into the bucket of paint, far past the ferrules, swung it back, overloaded, to the chair. One section of the broad lawn was now streaked with white. The paint would still be wet for the party tomorrow night. No one would be able to use the seat. Carol shook her head. On scaly branches, the oak leaves pitched up their silvery backs, like white caps at the summer house. Suddenly queasy, Carol stepped away from the roof's edge.

Dying, that's what she thought. Death. In block letters above her mother's pale head. *Death*, starring Edie Cameron. She half-listened to Kit and her father chat, something about Kit's own dad's elderberry wine.

He could be nice to her friends — comfortable — as if, instead of his distant self, he were a father who played team sports with his children, and sat on the edge of beds for chats when times got rough. She knew precisely how he would come off at the party: princely, a regular guy, and then, afterwards, he'd say something lacerating: "You had an ugly look on your face all night." Or, "You need to learn how to walk." Talk. Chew. Something.

She just smiled when her mother dreamed up this graduation party business; just smiled when Edie started the guest list in her new, choppy handwriting. They would come, those children of her parents' friends, though they were not Carol's friends, and she would not have hesitated to point out the fact to Edie before.

"Do you suppose you could get Carol for me, Kitty?"

Kit held out an imaginary pinafore, dropped a curtsy. "One moment, please," she said.

His nasal laugh, Hh-nh! Like the fizz from a bottle of soda.

"What do you want, Dad?"

"Would you come here, please?"

He squinted against the sun. With curled-back lip exposing upper gums, jaw hanging, he reminded Carol of one of Norman Rockwell's hicks visiting the city for the first time. She had seen photographs of herself wearing the same idiotic expression, awful, incongruous, that generic exposed look she knew from the faces of the school's retarded.

"You know I don't want you girls up there," Neal Cameron said. "You'll ruin the roof and come down into the porch."

Hairs on his chest speckled with white paint: arctic lichen. "We're already up here," Carol said. She looked off into the pines ringing the far end of the yard, dense as a forest, so private that you could not see into the neighbor's lot only fifteen feet beyond.

"I don't want you disturbing your mother."

"She told me it was all right, Dad." The words crowded past that rope of despair snaking towards her brain pan. Creep, she thought, he's worried about the damn roof so he tries to make me feel guilty about *her*.

Neal Cameron raised a hand and dropped it, signifying he found Carol too difficult to contend with, that he was too polite to make a scene in front of guests.

"The eternal power struggle," Carol murmured as she settled herself next to Kit.

"I like him, though. He's so different than my dad."

That was so obvious Carol considered Kit's statement offensive. Who would compare Kit's jowly father (pushed food around on his plate with a slice of bread, took an occasional punch at Kit and her mother) to Neal, who might be a jerk, but was still smart and charming and one of the best lawyers in town? She thought of her secret lover, Murray, a twenty-nine year old software salesman met during a presentation at school. "Hello, there," he said when she and the others filed out of the room. He took her elbow in an impressively proprietal way: a few weeks later she found herself between his tattersall sheets. Murray was handsome and smart, but he spoke of everything, including the two of them, in terms of the career-improvement seminars he attended. "We're not a small business, Murray," she told him. He laughed, okay, but lately she sometimes imagined how her parents would judge him — even if they did not know he was her lover! — and she found herself listening.

"Neal can be a bastard, too," she whispered to Kit. "Any time you take a screen off a window, the man explodes."

"Carol!"

She started: these days, everything signalled disaster. "What?" she called, then tried again; her voice had come out a whisper. "What?"

"Did you take a screen off that window up there?"

33

Kit stuffed a corner of the blanket into her mouth as though to gag her laughter.

"I don't believe it," Carol said, recovering from her moment of dizzy fear, the loose elbow, hollow belly. She called out in a sing-song, "Yes, I did, Dad."

"Lord. Well, put it back on."

She dropped her voice. "'Did you take a screen off the window?' 'No, Daddy, we just sieved ourselves through.'"

Kit laughed, which was enough to satisfy Carol for the time being; she put her cheek to the blanket and smiled at her friend. "Feels like a slumber party, doesn't it?" she said.

Vitamin D. The sunshine vitamin. She imagined her body injected with this honeyed fluid by millions of miniscule, irritating needles. The sun rose higher, felt hotter. She was Gulliver, shot full of the Lilliputian arrows. She shifted, front to back, back to front.

"I'm frying!" she cried. "Help, help!"

"Ugh, me, too," said Kit.

Carol propped herself on an elbow, looked down at Kit. Last year, she'd been planning on going to Stanford or Oberlin, but with her mother sick, she'd decided the state university would be a better, closer choice. Kit would be going to Madison. How she'd miss Kit!

"Listen, Kit," she said, "let's not go to college! Let's go to Maine! Open a candy store or something."

Kit, shut-eyed, rosy-cheeked, looked like one of the drowsy kids Carol babysat in junior high. Carol would have liked to give her a little kiss or a hug — something. "Hm," Kit said, "that sounds good."

Carol patted her friend's head in appreciation. "Sure, it does! We sit around all day eating doughnuts and Hershey bars. Get fat as hogs and not even care. Sell pillows stuffed with balsam needles, Swedish fish, fudge, almond bark better than Fanny Farmer's." Out the side of her mouth: "Say, girlie, do *you* know what cannibals give to their girlfriends on Valentine's Day?"

Boooo. I know, for the hundredth time."

"Farmers' fannies!" Carol hooted. She closed her eyes. "Isn't fanny an awful word? My parents seem to think it makes the mention of asses less offensive."

A little prayer for forgiveness welled-up: Almighty and most merciful Father ... Lately, the prayer came back to her often, so easily she had to stop and think what she was saying, *take care*. She didn't know that she believed in any of it, but the words, the action were a comfort, a small thing she could offer for her mother and herself.

She asked Edie once, before she got sick, if she believed in God. The two of them were folding still-warm sheets in the dining-room, a boring but not unpleasant duty which Carol hardly minded being roped into. Edie offered an answer bland as the Unity Village messages on TV — messages which Carol hated because, despite their irridescent stupidity, they made her eyes fill with tears, they gave her hope, made her want to change the world, something:

34

"Not all that business about salvation and so on," Edie had said, matching corner to corner, giving the length of yellow percale between herself and Carol a snap. "I think Christ meant we could have heaven on earth by treating others well." Like a color guard, she stepped towards Carol for the second fold, took Carol's end into her own hands, allowed Carol to pick up the new edge. They were ready for the third fold when Neal Cameron, coffee cup in hand, entered the room, sighed at the piles of laundry on the dining table.

"I don't believe like your dad," Edie said. Carol put the question to him, then, lightly, did he believe in Jesus, Jesus dying for our sins and all?

"Of course I do!" he said, eyes wide, revealing more canthus than Carol wished to see. She was touched by his naivete, wanted to comfort him almost, but she was angry, too, at such blind and invisible faith. She had thought: if I were going to believe such nonsense, I'd really believe it; I'd let it knock me dumb and silly and out of the race. There wouldn't be anything else *to* do.

The sweat dripped down the sides of her rib cage, making her skin tingle. She moved into a half sleep. She had lost the car keys along a road where everything was car keys, baskets and baskets of them. There was one particularly clever basket with a top —

"Carol," Kit said, "why would we want to go to *Maine*?"

Carol rolled over onto her back. The sun came hot pink through her eyelids and that feeling of transparency shocked her, was almost an insult; she should have been made of sterner stuff, not something that let in the light of an object ninety-three million miles away. She opened her eyes and looked out into the trees; everything had a shocked look to it, shocked, blanched, disjointed.

"Maine?" she said. "Because it's too damn hot here."

* * *

"My God!" The Carol in the mirror puckered her slightly sunburned face, ripped off the creamy knicker set (new), and used it to towel off her damp underarms. She was still sweating from a run up the street to the phone booth. An answering machine, something else new, had told her Murray was out, but would get back to the caller as time permitted! Carol left the phone dangling from its cord, hanging like a small choked animal.

She pulled on a pink jumpsuit, a present from Edie two birthdays back — one pocket, torn, revealed the suit's original ruddy pink — and went down the hall.

"Mother? It's me." She knocked on the bathroom door.

"Come in." Edie was in the dressing room, fresh from a shower. The smell of her Shalimar filled the bedroom. No one smelled as good in Shalimar as Edie; it warmed to her like honey on biscuits: good enough to eat. But there were other smells to her mother, too. Morning smells. A smell Carol now knew came from sex. The sick smell that had ripened at the hospital, blanketed by the perfume.

Carol sat down on the chaise. Shyly, her head tipped to one side of the

35

back cushion, she sniffed. For years, the chaise had been the snoozing spot of the family cocker, had carried the dog's corn chip smell; but now the upholstery was new, its scent peppery. The chaise smelled of nobody. She ran her fingers along the quilting, the stitches which cut polished cotton into jigsaw pieces. Mrs. Boyers, the day-help, had left some tawdry book on the end table. A man and woman, skin tinged blue, kissed in — an arbor? A gazebo? — while, in the distance, something burned. Carol blotted up a tear with a corner of one of the book's pungent pages. The paper darkened, became almost brown.

In the dressing room, Edie rattled hangers — a funny, familiar sound. Before she had gotten sick, she and Neal had gone out so much! Carol loved the way the weekday Mother became an enchanted being in calf-lifting heels, bobbling earrings, tropical lipstick: a creature who bent to kiss her tv-watching brood good-night with greater tenderness than usual, as if she sensed her own aura and used it well while it lasted.

Edie Cameron poked her head from the dressing room. "What's happening downstairs?"

"Nobody's here, yet."

"I want you all to have fun now. I told Daddy two drinks a piece. He's to be the only bartender. I hope no one will abuse the privilege." She paused, added, "But I'm sure all your friends are nice."

Downstairs the doorbell rang. Once, then twice. Carol wandered over to her mother's dressing table and lifted the heavy glass stopper from a cool and heavy bottle of cologne. She meant only to press the bottle against her wrist, leave a circle of scent, but the glass mouth slipped, and chill, heady stuff ran down her arm, soaked her shirt sleeve. Quick, she slicked the arm along her neck, scrubbed the wet cloth of her shirt against the jumpsuit; and, caring less about the cargo of perfume she would bear the rest of the night than her mother's seeing the sloppiness, mopped the wet bottle across the seat of her pants until it was dry.

The family dog wandered out of the dressing room, sniffed at Carol, then backed away: Carol, in Edie's perfume, was a stranger.

"Are you coming down, Mom?"

"Pardon?" Edied cracked the door of her dressing room wider. The mirrors reflected bone, bright incisions across her chest.

You kept yourself in readiness for this, like a driver prepared to avoid accidents by stepping on the gas, not braking. Carol smiled, did not look away.

"Are you coming down?"

"Later." Edie looked furtively towards the door as she struggled into a pair of panty hose. Worried I'll come in, Carol thought.

"Do you need some help? I can help."

"No, no. No, I'm fine."

* * *

36

Downstairs, Neal Cameron stood on the screened porch, explaining to the boys the virtues of Scotch while he mixed his "green monsters" (a liqueur/ice cream combination) for a group of girls. Comfortable, Carol thought, and was pleased, relieved.

"Did you check on your mother?" Neal asked when the others had carried their drinks away from the makeshift bar.

"She told me you'd be up."

Neal sniffed the air, smiled. In her cowboy boots, now, she could top him, but she knew he still saw her as a child, conceived of the excess scent as a little girl's dress-up. "I hope we're not making a big mistake allowing the booze," he said. "They're a good group. Seem to think quite a bit of you, too."

Carol fished a beer from the tub of ice. She could not afford to get rattled again tonight. The last time they had gotten *close* to close had been a disaster: he'd told her to sit down next to him on the porch, to talk. He kept losing the thread of the conversation, she thought he was upset. She thought, this is it, we're finally going to talk about Mom. Then she discovered he was listening to a ball game, had a transistor radio wire stuck in his ear! Sit down, sit down, he said when she got up to go. He had even pulled at her hand, but she had felt so betrayed all she could do was grin. Grin and back away.

Now the doorbell rang and she escaped to answer it. He never even told her her mother was dying. She learned the news from her brother, over the phone; people at school, strangers, knew before she did. Oh, she hated the way the real loss (her mother, her *mother*, for Christsakes!) was mixed up with the soap opera, *Medical Center, Marcus Welby*. Before the operation, Edie had shamed Carol by saying, in her most authoritative hangman's voice, such banalities as, "They took one look and sewed him back up." And that was just what had happened to her.

Carol let the new guests wander past, pointed them towards the back of the house. They were attractive, these children of doctors and bankers and clubwomen — attractive in their chinos and polo shirts. They smiled, revealing teeth straightened to the same orthodontic straightness as her own. Friendly, but not her friends. Susan Daly. Randy Beauvoir, so priggish his beauty seemed a mistake. Then there was the chubby son of her mother's best friend. Carol knew a story he'd invented about her, something hideous with herself tied to a bed as the main, dizzying image. She'd cried over that; now she just smiled her hello. "Gimme five!' the boy said, and she did.

Up the walk came Kit — whose own dad sold novelty items (lurid plates showing local history, goofy bumper stickers) — to gas station gift shops. "Oh, Kitty!" Carol cried. Crescents of pale flesh below Kit's eyes seemed the only area of relief on the girl's sunburned face. She looked like one of Hollywood's crazed and shipwrecked sailors; as if even the growth of her eyebrows would cause her pain. And there was something else.

"Here, here," Carol said, pulling her friend to the kitchen.

"He hit Mom," Kit said with a sob. "For no reason at all. He hit her with a box of tin foil, right in the eye!"

Carol moved to pat Kit's back, but Kit, managing a smile of apology, ducked her burned flesh away. "Oh. Sorry," Carol said. "Is she okay, your mom?"

"She acted like it was no big deal. 'Go on, now, and have fun at the party.'"

With the refrigerator door as a screen, Carol poured them each an orange juice glass of Scotch, which they downed, noses plugged.

"Ggrrhh!" Kit said, eyes watering from the liquor. Carol laughed, poured them each another half glass. She was comfortable in the kitchen, amid the island clutter of baskets and antique butter paddles, her mother's prized cigar form. Oddly, the kitchen was tidier since Edie turned it over to Mrs. Boyer: no more notes stuck here and there, no more boxes of items to be returned to the store, or vitamins meant to be taken.

"Let's just stay in here," Carol said, resting her head against a cabinet. Kit pushed a bowl into her hands. "Party," Kit said, "party."

At the sight of food, the guests let out an hoorah, as if they had been hired for a chip and dip advertisement. "Amazing," Carol said to Kit, who burped and pointed at Neal Cameron; he could have been performing tricks, considering the crowd he had gathered about him. Carol stepped to his side. He smiled.

"Get Mom now," she whispered in his ear. "Now is perfect."

She attached herself to a collection of shoulders and arms on the lawn and tried to pick up the topic of conversation: college, the doctoral programs in English at Ann Arbor and Stanford. She pressed her nose more diligently to her can of beer and appeared throughtful between sips. The skin of her brow contracted in a serious but not uncomfortable wedge. Alcohol helped you remember your body; your very limbs gained extension from their befuddlement.

Someone on the porch greeted her mother. Carol turned to wave.

"I don't think I'll come out," Edie called. "You just stay with your friends. Daddy's getting me a drink." She was wearing the cherry red pants and sweater set Carol bought for her after the operation, but she had shrunk away from the clothes in the months since. "I just want to look," she called. "Everything looks wonderful."

Carol was relieved Edie did not call her over. Edie might have made a little face to indicate perhaps Carol was drinking too much, too fast. But maybe not. In her junior year, Neal and Edie returned from a party and found Carol and a boyfriend smashed on rum, the counter littered with lemon peel, sandy with sugar. Carol and the boy were supposed to be at a function called "The Sweetheart Formal." Their lips were puffed with kissing. The boy's curly hair stood on end. Edie had said only: "You better get your dress ironed again"; Neal said nothing at all.

So maybe now Edie wouldn't acknowledge that guests not bold enough to go up for drinks beyond the Camerons' limit made trips to coolers in their cars, smoked joints in the lilac bushes at the side of the house.

From behind her, a voice said: "Old man Cameron didn't even know I'd been up there four times, man."

"Hey, this is my fifth!" said someone else. David Meyers. Shushed by those seeing Carol nearby. Carol pretended she had not heard, but her cheeks flushed with anger. Here her dad was trying to be nice, and they made him out the fool. As if he didn't know how many drinks they'd had!

"You enjoying the summer, Carol?" David Meyers asked.

"It's still *spring*, Dave," said David Stokes. All these David's. David's, Tom's, Steve's. "It isn't summer until the twenty-somethingth. Don't rush it, okay?" David said.

"Right," said Carol. Usually she hated a niggling correction, but not tonight, not in this instance. David left for Yale in the fall; she supposed he was scared, felt the future careening towards him like a box from the sky.

"Excuse me," Carol said.

In the porch's yellow bug lights, Neal and Kit's faces appeared jaundiced, unfamiliar. "So he's got to turn the thing back to Carol and me when we leave," Kit was saying. Neal nodded. The radio play. They were talking about the radio play, Carol thought. She scooped another beer from the cooler.

"This playing bartender has its disadvantages," Neal said. "All this booze around, if you're not real busy, you might end up on your fanny."

Carol smiled and looked down the table to Kit — spreading cheese on a Triscuit and trying to hold in her laughter. Carol sidled up to her. "Kitty," she whispered, "Kitty, dear, you're not going to end up on *your* fanny, are you?"

Kitty snorted, stuffed the cracker into her mouth as if it were evidence.

Neal Cameron smiled. "I think I missed something," he said.

Might *he* be getting a little looped? She had never seen her father drunk before, but her mother sometimes told a story about walking him around and around the block one night after he'd been drinking martinis. Twenty-five years ago. Her mother always ended the story with a little laugh, and said, "Were you obnoxious!" Carol didn't know whether the story told too little, or too much, but it made her uncomfortable.

Out on the lawn, people began to dance — slow drifting movement which seemed to have little to do with the music, everything to do with touch.

"Kitty," Carol said, "I think it's time for a chip trip." She aimed for her mouth, but the beer missed, dribbled down the front of her shirt.

Kit grinned woozily. "I'll pass on the chips. I don't think I could handle anymore chips."

"You ladies keep an eye on things while I check on Edie?" Neal Cameron said.

Carol nodded.

Coming towards them: Randy Beauvoir, the prig. BB, they called him, the Beauvoir Beauty. His and Carol's parents had summer homes near one another. The summer before, Carol and Kitty sometimes got Edie Cameron's binoculars out and marvelled, hysterical, over the boy's torso as he rigged his boat before races. Randy Beauvoir. They once threw their swimsuits at him when he sailed by. He pretended not to see.

"He's heading straight for you," Kit said, and lay her head briefly on Carol's shoulder. "I'm not — I think I'm going to puke." She tottered towards the door into the house.

"Kitty!" Carol called, but she was gone.

Randy Beauvoir stopped in front of Carol, a soldier reporting for duty, white shirt flat to his chest, posture perfect. Drunk.

"You want to dance?" he asked. Orders from home, Carol thought. She crooked a finger, indicating he should lean close. "Can't," she whispered, and did a few sloppy steps to illustrate the shape she was in. He rubbed his nose with the back of his hand, smiled.

"You don't look so hot yourself, Randy. You thirsty?"

"Sure, why not?"

"Oh boy, Randy, old Randy, I'll bet we could make something real good, Randy." Delightful, this using his name; as if she managed to rob him, yet he could make no objection. "Randy, Randy!" A stiff rum and Coke for each, mixture sloshing over the side of the glass and down her hand. Behind the sweetness she licked from her fingers, the taste of perfume.

Randy Beauvoir leaned against the porch wall, his damp skin catching the bug lights: gold. Carol steered him towards her old swing set. She caught the movement in the crowd, Joe to Tim to Alexis. Randy Beauvoir's friends —everyone at the party was his friend. How queer: her party, his friends. She stepped in front of Randy Beauvoir, put her arms around his neck, but he got to her first, kissed her hard.

Carol backed away. "You always think you're better than everybody," he hissed. Who was he frowning at? Her? His grinning friends. She sat down on the glider. The swings had disappeared who knew when or to where? Randy Beauvoir sat down opposite her, and, knees bumping, they kissed around the vertical bars of the glider. His eyes were pretty and brown and sad. She sang him a wobbly version of one of the songs her mother always sang on long car trips:

Oh, would you like to swing on a star
Carry moonbeams home in a jar —

Murray, when she first met him, sang her a song about how she was younger than springtime. She cried, even though Murray was very drunk, because the song was so pretty and she remembered it had made her mother cry, another time, when some old musical was on TV.

"You're an angel, do you know you're an angel?" Carol asked Randy Beauvoir. She hung by her knees from the swingset's crosspiece, kissed his ankles, and her face grew heavy and numb with blood. When she righted herself, he pulled her close, whispered: "There sure are a lot of people here."

Carol clicked her fingers. "You look like Superman! Like the guy who plays Superman."

"Christopher Reeves. I know. I mean, a lot of people have told me that."

She ran her finger along the tender shelf of his lower lip. "Come with me,

40

but be quiet. We don't want to start a run on the house."

They kissed all the way down the hall, stopping only once for a brief dance around the kitchen. "Now, shh!" she said as they passed near the bottom of the stairs. She held up a finger and smiled, upperlip sticking to her gums. "Jesus! I can't get my lip down!" She giggled. "When I'm drunk ..."

Randy Beauvoir bent over, laughter coming through his nose in small explosions. "Shh! Shh!" She thumped him on the back. "You're going to get me started, now, shh!" He straightened, face contorted. "*Vaya conmigo, señor.*" She inclined her head towards the door to the den. "Zee casbah."

The boy bowed. "Ta-dah!" he said, and stepped inside; but, then, just as quickly, he was back in the hall. Carol raised her shoulders, dropped them, waiting for a clue. When he said nothing, she looked for herself:

In the den, the reading lamp lit the big red chair she and her brother fought over for years. Neal Cameron sat on the couch. Sniffling, head hanging so far forward the nape of her neck was exposed, Kit leaned into his shoulder.

Neal nodded to Carol, pressed one finger to his lips for silence as with his free hand he stroked Kit's head.

They'd all learned to do things quietly in the last months, despite what they were feeling. Carol stepped back into the hall and closed the door. Quietly. She leaned against the door. Even her breath seemed too loud.

"Carol." Randy Beauvoir put his hand on her shoulder. She jerked away. She ran. Down the hall, out the kitchen, through the garage.

Off to the side of the drive, the gleaming Chris Craft they would take to the summerhouse perched rakishly on its trailer. She stepped to its far side, heart pounding as if baying hounds and men with guns chased her. The snaps fastening the tarp to the gunwales popped under her hand. She hoisted herself into the boat's dark warmth. Too dark, too dense with the perfume. She surfaced, shaking her head like a swimmer, and laid a generous triangle of canvas open to stars: pinholes in the stage certain, she had always thought, chocolate chip done up in blues.

After a while, the guests began to trickle from the house and into cars. They'd had a good time. One couple leaned against the boat, moaning. She did not want to know who it was, but, at the same time, she couldn't stop herself from going through the guest list: Susan Daly and David Meyers. As David Stokes passed, he said, "Did you see her mom?" and his companion added, "Yeah, well, her old man looks like he's dying, too. He must have lost twenty pounds since Christmas."

Some random celebrant shook a bottle of beer and its spray crested high, splashed down into the boat and onto Carol's upturned face. She did not make a sound.

* * *

41

When she awoke, the night was whiter, more lunar, cooler. She stood, the breeze played about her, as if she were on water.

Kitchen door, locked. Front door, locked. Through the dense growth of lilacs and honeysuckle, chill with dew, she passed round the side of the house.

He was still up, sat in the middle of the backyard staring out into the trees. He turned slightly. The short sleeves of his white shirt blew wide about his arms. She took another lawn chair off the stack on the porch, unfolding it as she walked towards him.

The day they had gone to the hospital, together, to bring her mother home, they found Edie waiting in the hall, in a wheelchair. Her back was to them; Neal had signalled to Carol to stop. He had gone on, approaching his wife slowly, making a circle so wide it scarcely appeared he came from behind. Her father's wary dance, the wheelchair, its position in the linoleumed hallway, let Carol know her mother was dying, it was not just news.

Now her father tilted his moonlit head. Listening? It was very late, three or four at least. The sky above the dark line of trees shone phosphorescent, white-blue as Neal's shirt, hair. Soon the sun would come up in a blaze that would replace all this with ragged greens, hard edges, the ordained red of the outdoor cooker, daytime flowers with colors decisive as crayons. Soon.

She sat down next to him. Together, they stared out at the dark, deep impenetrable U of trees before them, as if watching a fire, the sea, waiting for something to come in.

LOCOMOTION

There's my husband, standing on the curb. I almost miss seeing him, and only have a chance, from the left lane of this one way street, to give a quick salute and smile.

My husband's face — my ex-husband's face — looks disapproving. He disapproves of me, he disapproves of me not. He is wearing the flannel shirt I gave to him two Christmases ago and is flanked by women. One? Two? Already I'm down the street and the rearview mirror is useless. There were, at any rate, people on either side of him. He was preparing to cross.

Seeing him in his life, standing on a curb and ready to cross, I feel almost wise, as if someone has lifted a complex scientific theory out of the muck of my misunderstanding and said, "Here, this is all there is to it," and, of course, I understand, I understand, I would have always understood.

There he was, crossing the street. Autumn leaves. Flannel shirt. He had, besides the disapproving look, a mainstream look which took me by surprise: my ex-husband crosses the street, meets the autumn day with his handsome jaw parallel to the ground, eyes watching for cars. He always managed to look both impressive and fairly ridiculous. Even his hair — wonderful curly stuff he beat into depressing wedges — seemed simultaneously a clown's wig, a terrible bird perched and ready to attack.

He stood only yards away from the spot where, last March, I sat on the cold curb and painted a small canvas of my car's front end: the dull black of the wheel well, silvered white and blue of church spire and sky, a bare-branched tree melting over the hood.

I was three-quarters of the way through that painting when, to my surprise, I discovered my face in the bumper's chrome. Before I could go on, I had to make myself invisible, find the cement and the faded grass behind me.

* * *

I was honking my horn just before I saw him. Usually, I'm not bad with a horn. A brief "nick" serves me nicely. Nick-nick to the person who backs out of a parking space without looking. Nick-nick to kids playing frisbee in the street. But I was gunning down the road to pick up my child (his child, our child) at the day care. Four o'clock, framing excuses for my lateness (a little sad-eyed "I was delayed at the doctors," "I lost my keys," "I hit" — no — "Someone hit my car, and though there doesn't seem to be any damage" — a good natured smile of relief — "I thought I'd better get the insurance information"). Some blue boat of a car started pulling into my lane, a pale blue car like an iceberg, sliding into the space I was moving into, the space which belonged to *me*. Oh, big blue car, did I, university instructor, American mother, maker of cookies for bake sales, HONK and give you the finger? I did.

Did my ex-husband see this? He always thought I drove too fast and changed lanes too often. Is that what the disapproving look was for? Or did he think I was going to be late picking up our mutual child? Or that I was driving too fast and that the child was in the car? Or, there goes that jerk, still driving too fast? Or, simply, there goes that jerk?

One always hopes for expansion, for others to be endlessly aware of one's multitudinous self. Keep things complicated. Consider love. He loves me, he loves me not; but, please, let's not get side-tracked. He was a great and gentle kisser; his eyebrows met in the middle and I needed to touch them there, often; I was particularly pleased to hold, through the miracle of love and marriage, his jaw in common property.

Notice I speak in the past tense, as if he were dead. You must remember he isn't, he's back there crossing the street, maybe now he's on the other side.

I do not remember relinquishing the rights to our life together. I can still say to my daughter, like a good divorced mom, "Sure, your dad is a sweetheart," or, "It was Benny who taught me how to filet a fish," but what I remember comes on like someone else's home movies. I sit and watch my past, I respond like any viewer. When the lights go back on, I stretch and smile awkwardly at the others and hope they'll be the ones to say the first word.

On down the street, I stop at a red light. I keep my brake foot hard to the floor, a paragon of responsibility. Next to me, there is an old and shrunken couple in a beige Chevrolet. Her thinning hair is bound with a gossamer of netting. He sits so small and low in the seat that only a slim band of his face shows between fedora and window sill. I admire the creamy lines of the man's gray hat, the pure old age of him and the woman, the fact of their intimacy in the car. I pronounce them man and wife. For my purposes, they have been married fifty-nine years, cannot be brother and sister, cousins or neighbors. Fifty-nine! Imagine such a habit of intimacy! I once read in *Time Magazine* that long-married couples exhibit similarities even in their blood samples, have tendencies towards the same diseases. I, too, feel such effects. I was married a mere seven years, have been divorced for two, yet it is still Benny's name which has dominion. It is Benny's name which rises to my lips, must be recognized, then erased, before I speak the name of my lover. There are times when I frown the frown that belongs to Benny, and, in a moment, even the bones beneath my skin feel tight with his displeasure.

Hurry up, someone honks from behind. Hurry up. I want to roll down my window, ask the old couple how they did it. Sex? Tolerance? Love? Indifference? But hurry up, hurry up. I move into the green with all the pace and caution of the old man and woman and wonder if this will help.

* * *

Nora is waiting for me on the day care porch. I am, indeed, late. All the other children are gone home. The teacher waves to me and steps inside as

Nora comes running down the walk, a necklace of dry pasta, construction paper and string bouncing on her chest.

I reach across the car and open the door from the inside. "Hello, hello," I say, mustering my good mother courage. Nora scowls, scrambles onto the seat. Her sullen sorrow makes my heart swell. How can I have made so many mistakes already? "How about a smooch?" I say. She stands on the seat and presses her round face towards me. "On the button," I say, and kiss her on the nose I foresee growing to the small upturned cuteness of Benny's.

My lover, Tom, and I are big-boned, big-headed. My ex-husband had ankles like a Rockette, fingers shorter than my own. People stare at my chubby, fine-boned daughter, at my lover and me. "Yours?" they ask, as if we might be kidnappers.

For a time, I tried to believe there had never been a father, it was a miraculous birth; but genetics' own mystery-show moves in with a suitcase of characteristics — and there are his eyebrows, his dimples, his smile, and I must love these things, these parts of him, as I love her.

I tweek the pompom on top of Nora's hat. Her cheeks are like those exotic Korean peaches they sell canned in specialty stores — white with a yellow-pink blush. I would like to be a mother cat and lick at them with my tongue, make her laugh. These days, if I cradle her in my arms, she cries, "That's for babies," and perches on my knee. When she was very small, I could hold her so close that we could breathe one another's breath.

"You know what today is?" I ask her.

"What?"

"Guess!"

"I don't *know*," she says between clenched teeth.

"The magic show!" I say. "Isn't that neat?"

She climbs up on her knees and rummages in the glove compartment. "I'm hungry," she says, her voice sliding into a whine.

"Okay," I say, "We'll get you something."

She's surprised. I am the great withholder, the one who bats away the dinner hour. "At a restaurant," she says firmly, looking at me out of the corner of her eye. Already, when she can't manage tears, she'll raise a shielding hand to her eyes as if it were all too much for her and she doesn't want you to see her pain. Tom tells me, yes, definitely, she did learn this from me. I make no comment. I'm secretly flattered by all similarities between us; the more she is like me, the more she is mine. The more she is mine, the better.

"Okay," I say, "A restaurant, before the magic show."

"Where there are ducks," she says, referring to "Old Brick," a hipply converted home on the river, where wild ducks scramble over the banks for crumbs and lay their eggs in the peony beds.

* * *

At the counter, they sell dry bread. I buy a bag as we go in, thus eliminating the possibility of going back on my promise to feed the ducks. Our waitress tells us her name is Debbie. She kneels at Nora's side and rumples her hair. "What's your name, cutie?" she says.

Nora looks to me for advice, assistance. "That's Nora," I say. "Do you want the quiche or a sandwich, honey?"

Nora chooses quiche and an eclair. I say to this Debbie, "Would you, please, bring her eclair with dinner?" Debbie disapproves. Treats are for later. She puckers her lips and little frown lines fork her forehead. She doesn't realize that this is one of my measures for a proper diet and a healthy attitude towards food. I started out a purist, honestly: no sugar, no snacks, no processed foods, but I found my chubby child swooping down on candies in the gutter, digging wads of chewing gum off the undersides of tables, developing exaggerated ideas about the charms of popsicles. I am now trying to normalize her relations with the world of Sweet, Debbie; I erred, but am trying to make amends.

You see, it takes forever for me to learn anything. It was just last March, five years past my MFA and a variety of art history tests in which I glibly analyzed "Nude Descending a Staircase," "Les Demoiselles d'Avignon," that I learned the cubists' lesson. I was almost finished painting the canvas of my car's front end when the weather grew suddenly very rainy and cold. I thought, I'll finish it from a photograph, but when I tried to take "the photograph," I discovered I needed not one but eight shots, that my painting was the combination of my roving eye: a look at the chrome, a look at the rectory across the street, a look at the hub cap, and so on.

I suddenly had a key to all those paintings of parts! I had eight photographs in my hand to reaffirm the lesson should it become dim. Wonderful!

Unfortunately, my new knowledge did not help me with my canvas. I don't know if it was the final working from the photographs or what, but the painting was a failure. I had hoped that the viewers' first impression would be one of pattern, then, pow, that dominant yellow shape would announce itself as "car." As it turned out, people frowned and said, "Now, *what* is that?" They saw the patterns, but not the subject matter. As for me, all I could see was my car's nicely rendered front end, some reflections, a tree and a building across the way.

"You know who I saw today?" I ask Nora.

"Who?" she says. She is putting a second pat of butter on her roll; while she works, knife laying on a bank of yellow, I slyly palm the remaining pats and stick them into the napkin on my lap. I smile mysteriously when she looks up. "Guess!" I say.

"Who?" she says, indignant. She hates guessing. I always forget.

"Your dad."

"I didn't get to see him," she howls. "You didn't let me see him."

I am rotten at soothing people; the most I can do is make promises or threats. "Do you still want to feed the ducks after we eat?" I say, combining my best efforts into one.

"YES!" she shouts, but my ugly expression quiets her. "You promised."

"Fine." I am killingly calm. "Fine. You settle down then."

"Where's more butter?" she asks.

"Hmm?" I say, mouth conveniently full.

"There was butter on that plate."

"Well, " I say, "There isn't now."

* * *

There's a bulletin board at the cafeteria where I usually eat lunch. This bulletin board announces the day's menu in white stick-pin letters. Every morning, someone brings out a stepladder and changes the menu. I have seen this done, or, perhaps, I have imagined this being done: because the sign is high on the wall, I have supplied a ladder; because the sign is changed daily, I have supplied a person; the person I have supplied is short, perhaps because I have thought of the reach which requires the ladder.

Burritoes, breaded perch, Manhattan chowder, and, sometimes, beneath the menu, a fact or quotation: "The average year round temperature in San Diego is 63°." "Tom Thumb and his wife, Lavinia Warren, were of identical heights, each measuring three feet, four inches." Marvelous, I thought, and hoped Lavinia was happy looking square into Tom's eyes. I confess to having, as they say, almost swooned the first time my lover lifted me up to him; the move from Benny's five-foot-ten to Tom's six-foot-three was a temporarily thrilling escalation.

Today the sign at the cafeteria read, "It is harder to hide those feelings we have than to feign those we lack." I secretly copied this down on my napkin and slipped it into my pocket. Cheap stuff. Transparent as hell. I felt it was one of those random pieces of information which I should take to me, and, perhaps, if I held onto it long enough, it would incubate, hatch into some true knowledge. It would perch in my soul and make me clear as an x-ray with x-ray eyes.

* * *

It's been over two years since I stood in the doorway of our bedroom, drying a pan, and said to napping Benny of my soon-to-be-lover, "The new guy in the department really reminds me of you, Benny. He's really wonderful — he's smart and kind of quiet and he even looks a little like you. He's really wonderful."

Someone would have had to hit me over the head with a two by four to shut me up. Even I didn't know, still don't know, if Tom reminded me of Benny, or if what I was actually saying was, he reminds me of the way I used to feel about you, help, do something.

Benny grunted. He said he didn't think he wanted to meet any more of my "school friends," and pulled the cover up over his head.

Two weeks later, I called my mother. "I want a divorce," I said, and began to cry. I thought, perhaps, that she would cry, too. She was quiet for a very long time, her breath ticking on the other end of the line. Her silence

47

made me feel so ashamed of myself that I was almost hopeful.

"Well, Kay," she finally said, "quite honestly, I always thought you were too smart for him."

Do not misunderstand, I knew my mother was capable of saying such things; still, I was hurt, both by her lack of surprise and the invitation to disloyalty. "If you're going to say that, I'm getting off," I said.

"Now, hold on," she said, and I did. "Does this have anything to do with the new fellow in your department?"

She was almost five-hundred miles away. I had mentioned Tom to her, casually, once. And what had I said? Something about his sculpture, his nice voice. Did I alter my life because a man sat down next to me and asked, in a voice that made my metal chair vibrate, "Would you like a cup of coffee?"

"Is it him?" Mother asked.

"I don't know."

She cleared her throat. "Do you still love Benny?" she asked. I hated like hell for her to be my confidante, but I *was* the one who had called. "What do you think, Kay," she said, "Do you still love him?"

I said, "I was hoping you'd tell me I did."

* * *

Out on the river, the ducks breast the water, each of them the apex of a trembling V, as if ghost flocks follow behind. They seem to be always at rest, meditative. I never see how they get anywhere, but when they clamber up the bank on their comic orange feet, shake themselves like puppies, I understand that they do hard work under the murky surface, webs pulling back water, shaping direction.

Piece by piece, Nora throws her crumbs to the ducks. "Mom-mom-mom-mom-mom," she cries when they come too close, when they boil about her ankles.

The wind coming across the river is cold. I button my jacket all the way up. I say, "Let me help, too, Nora," and begin throwing great handfuls of breads out onto the water.

"Save some for me," she cries. "That's too much. Save some for me."

"It's getting late," I say. "The magic show will be starting. We have to go." Three reasons. One. Two. Three.

* * *

The auditorium is immense, a jumble of boxes, like the remains of an elegant woman's shopping spree. The ground lights shine on the pale walls, making the dusk seem darker, the hour late. We squeeze through the heavy doors with the rest of the crowd, funnel into the big lobby with its ten foot paintings, full grown *ficus benjamina*, and chic austerity.

Rabbits are extracted from hats and newspapers and boxes of candy. Nora knows so little about what's possible and what isn't that she doesn't discriminate between spectacle and tricks: why shouldn't a handkerchief dance in the air? why not have a small yellow bird appear when you clap your hands? She taps me on the arm and whispers, "Are they going to share that candy, Mom?"

The program notes say that the magician's number one assistant is his wife. She is the queen of the dancers, the one who gets sawed in half, who is offered the gloved hand at the end of the tricks; it is she who wears the chief's headdress in the Indian number. Any one of the women could star in any or all of her spots; there is no skill involved in the help she offers the magician, but it is she who is designated "wife" and I am sure that I am not alone in watching for the secret glance. In all her tacky splendour, her stewardess glamour, I envy her her public position of beloved.

The magician's gestures are enormous and stylized. His voice booms and cajoles. He is slimy-slick and despicable, but no one can step onto the stage with him without appearing a fool. He pours a volunteer a glass of liquid from a wrapped bottle. "What's it taste like?" he asks the man.

The man hesitates. "Weak Coca Cola?"

"'Weak Coca Cola,' you say? 'Weak Coca Cola'! Well, ladies and gentlemen, my young friend made an interesting guess, but an interesting guess is not a correct one, for as you can see" — he cracks the bottle with a small wooden mallet handed to him by his wife — "what the bottle contained *was*" — a flash of white fur is drawn from the broken container — "Essence of Bunny Rabbit!"

The audience laughs and claps in delight. I check Nora for a reaction and see that she is confused. "He said the man drank bunny juice," I tell her.

She wrinkles up her nose and smiles. "Bunny juice?" she squeaks, "that's funny, isn't it, mom?"

I could weep with shame over the way she courts me. "If you like it, I like it," I say, and give her an awkward squeeze over the armrest. She smiles and begins clapping.

The dance troupe comes on in red, white and blue to perform "The Bicentennial Salute": glittering women kicking up fishnet legs, banners, a used carlot's share of bright U.N. flags, louder music, plumed horses, trick dogs, and the magician talking faster and faster, moving about the stage like a Hollywood commander in the midst of battle.

When all this stops, the chaos turning to sudden order, the noise to a theatrical silence, and I realize that an elephant — a small earred, sequin-capped and caped Indian elephant, its trunk fanning in slow motion — has somehow materialized on stage, I feel neither more nor less confused and amazed than I do all day, every day.

The lights go on for intermission, and far down front, in the good seats, I see the back of a head which looks like the head of Benny. Whether it bends to the left to what must be a small child, or to the right to the curly-haired head at its side, I cannot see the face.

I imagine that if I saw myself from behind, I would look very much like that curly-haired woman, that I might, as she does, lay my head on the unseen

49

shoulder of the man whose-head-looks-like-the-head-of-Benny. I rise up out of my seat and stand, as if stretching my legs. I try to see a face, to detect the top of a child's head in the left hand seat, but I am dealing with a conspiracy of angles. Other people turn in their seats and scan the audience behind them, but those heads down front are in their own world; they are there for each other, and have no need to announce themselves to anyone else.

Nora tugs on my skirt. "What do you see, Mom?" I look down at her, and it's true, her head would not show over the top of the seat, not at all.

"What do you see?" she asks again.

"Okay," I say, and begin pulling on my jacket. "Let's go, kiddo-kiddo."

"It's not over!" she cries. "I want to stay!"

"We're leaving." I take her up in my arms, grab her coat and pass awkwardly over knees. Excuse me, excuse me. Nora screams at the unfairness and people turn. I squeeze her arm tight, whisper in desperation, "I'll buy you an ice cream if you're quiet."

We move out into the dark of the parking lot and away from the halo of the auditorium. The cold blue lights here are so high and shed so little light they seem dull stars, more ornamental than utilitarian.

"You're hurting my hand," Nora cries, "go slower."

"You want to ride?" I bend for her to climb onto my back. I kiss her fingers over my shoulder.

"So, did you like that?" My voice booms in the dark of the little car. I sound almost like the magician. "Wasn't that fun?"

"Yes," Nora says, and sniffles. "And there were bunnies and the man drank bunny juice."

"But not really," I say, and back the car out of its space. "Not really."

It is good to be leaving the magic show, to be driving past these sleeping herds of cars, soft lights overhead winking on hoods and windows. I press on the accelerator, then find myself braking in confusion, arm shooting out to shield my child.

A great wall of gray, fold upon fold of gray, fills the road. A young man steps into the lights between us and this vast grayness. He raises a small baton and signals for me to stay, turns, taps the shape in the road with the stick — once, twice, three times — and towards us turns an enormous head, a patient eye blinking among the folds of gray. Like a lover touched at precisely the right moment, in precisely the right place, the great trapezoidal flaps of skin which are the ears do their shimmering tremble, and then the whole is set in motion.

"You stopped too fast," Nora says and begins to cry. "You did that too fast."

"Look," I whisper to her. "Look at that," and she rises in her seat, and we both watch, breathless, as the magician's elephant lumbers across the road and into the dark.

HONEY

is what he is calling her, is what she can never believe. Honey. Just like she is his wife, a woman full of grace, instead of thirteen and a little sweaty under her t-shirt. She has no name for him. Except Everything. And his own name, which jangles her blood and makes air a traitor to her lungs. She thinks of him in biology class, him passing through her alveoli and into her bloodstream. She is an exceptional student. An ES, the school says, but he does not know that.

He leans back against the inside of the door of his car. They float somewhere near a factory crystalized in its own pale dust. The houses spinning on the edge of this world share the dust. The people who live in the houses work at the factory. At the end of the day, they come home bisque. They take baths. They lead secret lives in their glad yellow and pink and brown skins. They eat scalloped potatoes with ham. They have sex with their wives. But when they blow their noses: dust.

She thinks the factory is wonderful, its storage towers good as turrets anyday, but she doesn't understand why she and he are still there. Maybe because he knows the factory is wonderful! *That* would be wonderful. But she suspects they are where they are because it is one more place where no one else is.

There is a steak house between the car and the factory. She could cover it with her thumb if she didn't suspect he would ask what she was doing. Some people once took her to that steak house. It was supposed to be funny to go there. Ants were flowing in the front door. She entered with ants. They flowed past the booth where she and the others sat. They were like little bits of type. While the Greek man who ran the place explained pastitsio to the others, she stared at the sticky table and tried to compose something filled with the letter I.

Honey. He pulls her close to him. Their clothing creaks. You are so beautiful, he says as his chin rakes across her forehead. It has not been long since he shaved, she can tell because there is a soapy tang to his neck. Still, his beard is already rough. If she tilts her eyes up just a little, she can see: so many follicles full of thick, frightening hair that his skin seems a little gray.

He does not work at the factory. He goes to college. Two textbooks lie on the back seat. Music appreciation. Life science: as full of fleshtoned pictures as her fourth-grade health book. She supposes his college is a very bad one. With its sleek, low lines, she thinks it resembles a motel. Rich people go there, her father said once, the kids who can't make it anywhere else.

If her father knew she was sitting in this car with this young man he would kill her. He would pick her up by the hair and slam her into the wall the way he did the first time he saw them together, her father running out of the grill, yanking her away from the young man as surely as the young man had yanked her out of her life.

She sees herself, tan shorts, orange top, her father in his greasy apron, just like somebody took a photograph of the moment.

Her lover's lips are full, but flat, with an almost silvery pall to them. Beautiful. She touches them. They are warm and dry, like her dog Dooley's nose when Dooley's feeling sick. She presses her cheek into his jacket, glad they are not going anywhere. Sometimes, he drives his car so fast she thinks he means to kill her. She imagines them leaving the sky smeared with the car's beige paint.

She has not told him, she will never tell him, but a few days ago, while walking the dogs in the cemetery, she caught sight of her bare legs flashing on a glossy-faced piece of granite, and thought of his beard: how the skin shines where he shaves. She was frightened. She let out a little scream, which she transposed into jubilance for the sake of the couple walking up ahead.

If she told him this, he might notice even more how she is not him.

He's sorry he hasn't called all week, he says. She nods and laughs. That's okay, she says, the words hanging above her head in a cartoon bubble, the space around each letter a flat white. She would like to lasso that bubble and drag it down, but when she is with him, she seems weak.

He sighs. His nails are chewed so deep the crowns of his fingers resemble blind puppies. He reaches with these fingers for a cigarette. Smoke curls from the factory, the cigarette, his fingers curl around the steering wheel and he places his head between them. Soon he'll wedge his tongue into her mouth and his knee between her legs, but for her, that insistence will happen far away. Between his insistence and herself, she will erect a tenderness, a place of repose, cozy as the little house she fashioned beneath the basement stairs: a lamp, an old rug over the suitcases, a dish of wrapped, hard butterscotch that dissolved slowly on the tongue.

He doesn't understand that just last summer she was still playing with dolls.

He doesn't understand anything about home, her six brothers and sisters, the rabbit hutches in the backyard. His parents have a swimming pool he told her once, smiling a secret kind of smile, as if she were supposed to be impressed. She was not impressed. She knew what to be impressed by: his beauty, the baby rabbits, despair. The night before, her dad brought an old man home with him from the grill. Her mother told her, "Now don't stare," staring at the man and her husband coming up the walk. The old man had skin like cobwebs. He sat down at the plate decorated with golden sprigs of wheat, the plate she liked to eat from herself. He piled more and more food on his plate: mountains of mashed potatoes, decks of meat loaf, corn. He ate his potatoes with slices of bread, folding bread around the mound on his plate in the same way her mother used a piece of paper towel to pick up one of the dogs' messes. He ate and ate and ate. Her father and mother talked — just a little, but more than usual, as if the room would sink and all of them with it if somebody did not provide some sound. (She watched from beneath her eyelashes, missing the man's face, but getting everything of his hands — which were strong and white and pointed as incisors. Before he got up to go, he wiped his plate with a last slice of bread, around and around, until the plate was clean, the gold sprigs of wheat revealled once again.)

She rolls her window up, although it is not really cold out. Rolling up her window is something to do. If she could, she would tidy up the car, wipe down the dash with a Kleenex, vacuum the bits of gravel and cigarettes and paper off the floor.

He says maybe he's going to join the service, he needs to get straightened out, what does she think?

She thinks she will fit her back tighter to the seat. Perhaps this announcement means she will have to have sex with him. The service? she says. In the funnies, there is one about The French Foreign Legion. And Beetle Bailey. She tries to imagine him gone. Her Uncle Brian — she never knew him really — died in the war with Viet Nam. In the photograph of him which her aunt used to keep on the tv, his face looked buffed, almost as if he didn't even have a beard. Now her aunt is married again; the picture has disappeared.

If there were a war, he could die in it. Then she could love him forever, but not have to be with him. She could go back to her friends. She could laugh with the boys in her class at school. No. It wasn't fair. She had no choice. She looked at him and even while she was backing away, her heart was going out to meet him, betraying her fast as the speed of light. Impossible to imagine.

She turns sideways, offering him only her profile. Maybe, if she holds very still, she can disappear; invisible enough, she'll just slip inside sometime while he's not looking, she'll fill him up, he'll be sleek and satisfied; but if he tries to come on to someone, she'll be there, she'll wave from behind his eyes and ruin everything.

He heard she was with someone else, he says, at the movies; but all she has to do is tell him it isn't true, and he'll believe her.

She feels a little sick, like she did last spring when her parents came to the music program, and she knew, as soon as she was on stage, that she was going to ruin her solo — a feeling like being hit on your crazy bone, only all through her body. Why doesn't she ever ask him about things she's heard? Things he said about her? Things he said to her?

He rolls his window down, runs his fingers through his hair. "We could get married, honey," he says. "Would you like that?"

Grinning, ashamed of the grin, she leans over and pulls up her knee socks. Once, her criticized her because of a little roughness on her knees, there. There. She cannot straighten. She presses her fingertips to the lucky pennies in her loafers, trying to keep the moment from moving on — so she doesn't have to be just thirteen and pretty and alone again with the insistence of his teeth, his hands, his legs and canny breath. She scratches at the face of Abraham Lincoln, freer of the slaves. She thinks of the old man, last night, lifting his bundles of potatoes to his mouth. His plate empty, then full, then empty again.

53

SILVER FOX

We roll out early. "It's a good twelve hours to Omaha," Kyle says, "and the sooner we get there the better!" He's all dressed by the time I get the water heater turned down. He's always like that: raring to go. The first time I saw him he came bouncing into Mrs. Lane's room. "Gloria Lane," he said, "if you and this lovely nurse of yours would be so good as to accompany me down the hall, I'll be so good as to accompany you back again!" Mrs. Lane had thrown a full can of 7-Up at me not ten minutes before and the fact that she was blind didn't hurt her aim, but she said to Kyle, sweet as you please, "If that's you, Kyle Carter, I'll come."

Kyle's little, but built nice, and has a smile that'd knock down a bridge. When he visited the old folks at the home, he left them all grinning.

"Betty, Betty, slow as confetti," he teases me. I just laugh. The dishes are clean. The sky is blue. I'm going on my honeymoon with a man handsome as a thrush in his brown knit shirt, brown pants, this belt with a tiny gold stripe running through it. Nobody needs to tell me I'm lucky. Kyle says no one would guess he's younger by eight years, but I know better. I take care of myself. I rinse my hair every two weeks the same as I have the last twenty years. First peroxide for the roots, then the wash, then the rinse. It was my first husband, Mike, that chose the color. Silver Fox. We were at Seaton Drug. "Her," he said, pointing to this gal they had smiling away on the bottle. And it worked. He seemed to believe I was less me, or more her, when I came out of the bathroom later that afternoon. Sometimes I worry they'll stop making my color, but my girl, Jean, says, "Don't worry, Ma, they make lots better products than that anyway," and she's probably right.

Kyle puts his coffee cup down on the table and bends over his watch, winding like there's no tomorrow. "Kyle," I say. He lifts his head, smiles. His face is a little shiny, he's so excited about the trip. "Not too tight," I want to say, "we only got the watch back from the jeweler's last week." But that might spoil things, so I just ask, "You're not feverish, are you?"

"No, Nurse Betty," he says. He always says I'm a nurse, even though I'm really just an aide. He talks real low like I'm not there: "Finally she gets off for a honeymoon and I can't get the girl out of the house!"

I giggle. "I'm going, I'm going," I say and trot down the hall to the bedroom.

I've never been to Omaha, but Kyle's got some house there we're going to sell. I didn't know anything about it till two days ago. The money from the sale's going to be a first anniversary present, he says; that's because he feels bad about not having a job. Not that I care. I've got this house paid for, and my job. We can manage, but he's got his pride. "The economy's bad," I always tell him. He had a good job before we met, right here in Nashville. He did something technical for one of the record companies, one of the big ones. Somebody got jealous, though, spread lies, and he got canned.

"First thing I'm going to get you," he calls down the hall to me, "is a new dog."

Alhasa's what I had when we met. Her name was Chita and she was as good a friend as a dog could be, but this bum vet cut the nerve that controlled her sphincters. Nothing to do, he said, but put her to sleep. I said forget that. I had to help her go, you understand, and it was no fun, but she was my friend seventeen years, and I see messes at work every day, so what the hell? She didn't last long. I come home one day and there was Kyle, sitting on the bed, looking about to cry. He took me out back and showed me this little grave he'd buried her in. I had to go to the doctor for some medication and Kyle stayed with me through it all. I guess I was as bad off as after Mike and Eddie died.

I been widowed twice, once by cancer and once by the bottle. "Two killers visited my house already," I warned Kyle, but nothing could stop him.

He dances into the room with this pen stuck between his teeth, like one of those people with a rose. "We can't sell the house until we get to Omaha, Betty!" he says, and twirls me around the room.

I seen him do this with the lady who runs the home where I work. She was acting like maybe he should leave the premises and he started dancing her around the lobby and all the old folks started clapping and she realized what a great guy he was, after all. She lets him come by whenever he likes.

"You just hold on a minute, Mr. Carter," I say to him, pretending I'm a little bit mad. "Have you got the thermos filled up? And the timers set for the lights?"

He nods. "How about the money belt?" I ask him.

He squeezes his eyes shut tight, slaps his head. "Oo," he says, "good thing you're here, Betty," and he pulls it out of the bureau drawer and fastens it around his waist.

I wish it were more than eight hundred dollars. When I told Kyle how much I'd got for the trip, he shook his head. "That's not enough for a real honeymoon, Betty!" he said. Then I think he figured out I didn't have more, so he said not to worry, once we got to Omaha and sold that little house we'd be rolling in the dough.

* * *

I know if I don't tell Kyle to stop in Paducah he won't. He's driving between seventy and seventy-five and the speed seems to nourish him. Kyle's a toast and coffee man, but I like a good breakfast. Fried eggs, bacon. In Nashville, we've got grits in most places, and I'll take them whenever they're offered. I always apologize about making stops on trips, but then Kyle says it's all right, all the trouble you've had, you deserve to enjoy what you can, Betty.

I'd like to be slim for him, but, damn, I wanted to be slim for Mike and Eddie, too. The young girls at the home, they'll eat a carton of yogurt or an apple for lunch. Can you imagine that? Kyle says I'd lose if I smoked, but I think of my Mike, lying in that bed — my big, strong husband looking like one of those squirrels the cats drag up on the lawn after a car flattens them.

"How about here?" I ask Kyle when I can make out the big chef that one place stands out front.

"Good as any," he says, and brakes for the exit.

* * *

"You watch," says Kyle, "it's the ladies that order the pie." We watch this one gal, all alone, wearing a suit like a man's. "Lemon meringue," she tells the waitress.

When the waitress comes over to us with our silver, Kyle drops his voice real low and asks, "Honey, you know any places that rent rooms by the hour?"

She's probably sixteen, with one of those faces like they have on the dolls little girls are so nuts about, you know the ones. She looks at Kyle, then me. Kyle can keep a deadpan, but I crack up. Then she gets it and laughs, too. "What do you folks really want?" she says, finally, and pretty soon I'm enjoying the patty melt platter and Kyle is telling me how long it takes for a good short order cook to prepare sixty breakfasts.

I'm just as happy Kyle keeps signalling for the girl to bring more coffee. I could stay all day in these cozy places. This fellow at the counter — big guy with a little hat on — he's got "The Paducah Shopper" in front of him, but I can tell he's listening in. People listen in lots when Kyle talks.

"You folks from Nashville?" he asks. I wait, to let Kyle answer, just in case he might judge the fellow suspicious looking or something; Kyle smiles. "That's us," he says, "so it's okay."

"Thought I noticed your plates," the man says, nodding out towards the parking lot.

We get to talking. The man grins and points at the shopper on the counter in front of him. "It says here you can send in two dollars and they'll send you title for a lot on the moon."

Kyle lifts up a little in the booth so he can see what the man is reading. "Now that'd be something, wouldn't it?" he says. "One of these days, they start sending people up there to live and you walk in and say, 'Why, I notice you built your new space grocery on that lot there, and I'm afraid I'll have to ask you to pay me a million dollars 'cause I'm the owner!'"

The man at the counter laughs and laughs. Kyle laughs, too. "Say, honey," he says to our waitress, "you got any more of them 'Shoppers' around?"

Just like he believes maybe we ought to buy one of the titles. I suppose it might look cute on a wall or something; but, I can't help feel a little bit jealous of the way he watches the waitress walk over to the stand by the door.

"Got to go to the little girls," I whisper.

56

Somebody else is in there, using the mirror, so I only get to peek at myself sidelong.

Kyle's by the register, chatting with the girl. A five dollar bill sticks out from under the cracker basket when I go back for my scarf. I run a quick tab and figure a dollar fifty would have been over twenty percent.

"What's that card I saw you giving her over there?" I ask on our way to the car. I smile, like I'm just getting a kick out of his cutting up, but you know better.

Kyle winks and opens up his wallet. He's got business cards in there, and one of them reads

TALENT, INC.

and gives a Nashville address.

"What's that?" I ask.

"A joke," he says, "can't you tell a joke?" He holds my door open for me. Always. I can't get over it.

* * *

"We're going to stay at The Red Lion," he says as we're skirting St. Louis. "We'll eat dinner at Maxine's. Lobster. Whatever you like."

I'm half-asleep, but that sure sounds nice. Lobster! The one time I ever had lobster was when Eddie took me to that Christmas party and we had our choice, Kansas City steak or lobster. My one hand's pillowing my head against the window, but I reach over with the other and pat Kyle's knee. That's when I spy the nose of the police car sticking out from behind a weigh station.

"Kyle!" I say, sitting up real straight.

"No problem," he says.

The patrolman says hello, the way they do, like we're all friends. "In an awful rush there?" he says.

"Some folks are having an anniversary party for us up in Omaha, Nebraska," Kyle says. "We'd hate to miss out on all the excitement."

The officer looks in at me. "Your anniversary, too, ma'am?" he asks. I nod. He makes this little face that I don't quite know how to read, but it leaves me feeling sick all the same. We just sit there, real quiet, while he writes out the ticket on his clipboard.

I wait a few minutes down the road before I ask Kyle if it's true.

"What?" he says.

"About the party?"

"Well, it could be. I could let some of my buddies know we're coming into town, couldn't I?"

"Then there's not a party?"

"There just may be."

I let it drop. Kyle has a lovely voice, a little like Mel Torme, I think, and he sings while we drive across Missouri: "Moon River," "I Get a Kick Out of You," and early Beatles. He tells me about the house in Omaha. "The roof's not bad, but it needs paint. We'll give what they call a paint allowance. Knock off a hundred bucks or so."

"I'm glad you know about these things," I say, and I mean it. The coffee left in the thermos is luke, but we drink it down, both of us sharing one cup, just the way I did with Mike and Eddie. Since we'll be getting in awful late for a night on the town, we decide to stop at a Dairy Queen for a bite. When Kyle comes around to open my car door, he says, "Lobster mañana. Lobster *and* ice cream."

Kyle always eats his hamburger in three bites. I never really see it happen because his cheeks get so big when he takes that first bite, I figure I should look away. After that first bite, the bun is about a half moon. But you shouldn't try to change the ones you love. I know that much, so I just sort of bow over my food till I know the sandwich is gone, then I can relax and know he's satisfied.

"My daddy always told me, 'Buy land, land's the only thing that lasts," he says.

I nod. That's what Scarlett O'Hara's dad told her, too, and it was good advice. Where would she have been without land? Nowhere, that's where. "You want some of my fries?" I ask Kyle.

"We might even buy a little piece of something near home, once we sell this house," he says as we're getting back in the car. A semi roars past us, maybe on its way to Omaha, too. "Out there where we drove by last week?" I say.

"Rooster Hollow?" Kyle slaps the steering wheel with a hand. "You've got a good head on you, you ought to have been a business lady, you know that? Still could be."

"Too told to change," I say, and it's true. I'm fifty-two years old, and, with Kyle driving me along this blue-black road, everything beyond the window like water, I don't mind at all. I've had three good husbands and chances are I'll beat this one to the grave. If I'm lucky. I don't think I could bear to sit by and watch another one die. And I'm not so silly that I shiver to think of him remarrying, either. As long as he finds a solid sort of woman who'll treat him right and keep my house nice, it's not my place to complain.

* * *

In the night, all lit up, Omaha's prettier than I imagined. The big buildings bunch together, coraled by the 480 bypass and the Missouri River. Altogether, they look like some big computer from a science fiction movie.

"Right below us," says Kyle, "and there's The Red Lion, see there?"

A great, hot lion's head glows on one of the big buildings. It makes me a little scared, to tell you the truth. I haven't stayed in a hotel since my senior class went to Washington, D.C., back in nineteen-forty-nine. Not that I figure I'd disgrace myself or something. Nothing like that., Anyway, I just smile and say, "Isn't that something?"

Kyle doesn't exit, though; he picks up speed. "I better call first, make sure we can get a room," he says.

He used to live near here, he says. The light of the telephone booth makes him look queer, like Eddie under the sun lamp, trying to get some color when he was dying. That scares me. I do a trick I learned long ago. I put a little hook around the thought of Eddie and Kyle and I tug the thought in another direction, hook it up to something else, in this case, the greenhouse across the way. It's not a whole lot better. What was pretty in that downtown isn't here. Here, it's dark, and the only light is from mercury lamps. The greenhouse is shabbier than any I've ever seen. But maybe it's nice in the day. Whenever I've been in a greenhouse, I've always thought the thing they needed was clean windows. Now just imagine what a beautiful thing it would be to look at all those plants under clean glass. I even start thinking about me and Kyle in there, with the moon up above, the two of us lying in among the plants and all.

Kyle surprises me when he knocks on the window. "No vacancies till tomorrow," he says, "but they'll put us up at Super Saver."

* * *

It's funny I'm disappointed about The Red Lion since I was scared to go there, but I am, like I've missed some chance. Still, The Super Saver is pretty nice, and we'll spend less staying there, so it isn't too bad. They've got some packets of coffee, complimentary, and I make us each a cup. We watch Carson for a while. The t.v. is black and white, the first black and white I've seen in a long time, except when I watch the old movies, sometimes, they show up in black and white.

"Johnny looks tan, doesn't he?" I say. Kyle nods. He seems a little distracted. "You cold?" He shakes his head, which he's propped way back on the headboard, about as uncomfortable as you can imagine. "You going to call somebody?" I ask.

He sits up straight, and fast, and I edge back, a little scared by his moves. "Who'd I call?" he says.

"Some old friends. I don't know."

"They all moved away." He plumps a pillow and puts it behind his head. At least he looks more comfortable that way.

I go back behind the divider to make us some more coffee, but the two packets are all they provided. "I guess we can go see the house tomorrow?" I call.

The bed creaks out there. He changes channels. *Harry O*? I like It. I comb a hank of hair into an unfamiliar parting and check the roots. It's time. No getting around that.

"There isn't any house." Right next to me. How'd he get there so fast. I comb my hair down quick, and try to take in what he's saying. "Never was a house."

"Well, Kyle," I say, but the breath is knocked out of me. I stick my comb back in my vanity kit, and then I do the only thing I can do: open my arms to him.

59

"You're too good. You're too good," he says, and cries like a baby.

I stroke him, my hand going over the slick part of his hair, then the part the barber clips, then the nice neck, and the shirt. That shirt was Mike's. I get a little confused about where we are: Omaha. I make a map of it in my head. Right there, I tell myself, and surround the dot with yellow, just like they did in the atlas.

I feel sort of dizzy and sick and Kyle's pressing too hard on my leg, but I don't say anything. I know just what my kids would say, because they said it before, when I married Eddie: He sure pegged you for a ringer.

But it's not true. I didn't marry Kyle for a house. It's not like I even knew about it before we got married. It's like a dream more than anything. You go to bed believing one thing, then you dream something else, then you wake up and you're back to what you knew.

"We'll just go home tomorrow," I say, and he nods. Really, I feel kind of tender towards him, the way I felt when Mike confessed about some girl at work.

"Why don't you let me run you a bath, honey?" I say.

After he's in the tub, I undress. I've brought along a nightgown set Jean and her kids gave me last Christmas. It's pretty, but not foolishly sexy: pink with short sleeves and a Peter Pan collar.

The bathroom door opens and I can hear Kyle, on the other side of the divider, brushing his teeth, then shaving, the way he sometimes does when we're going to make love. I tie the bow under my collar and climb into bed. I smooth the blankets over my legs and read a little out of the Bible they've got there, right from the beginning.

I suppose it shows, how surprised I am, when he comes around the corner, all dressed in a clean shirt and wearing Ed's lariat tie with the chunk of turquoise on it. He laughs and snatches the money belt off the dresser, like a baseball player after a grounder.

"I'm hungry as a bear," he says. He laughs, but his eyes are pink, shiny, just like my boy Donny's used to be after a good cry. I'm hungry as a bear. When he says that, he sounds like one of the colored boys that used to work on our floor. They didn't fool me with their innocent ways, and neither does Kyle. He just leaves me depressed. But maybe he's right. Maybe we ought to go out. I start to pull back the covers —

"You just stay put," he says. He slips the money belt into his jacket. It disappears, cool as a ferret, like something he had nothing to do with. "I'm going out to the Colonel's and" — he gives me a real sweet kiss.

"Don't you want me to come?"

"You just get cozy," he says, and does something he does when he means private business.

"It's eleven-forty-five," I say.

"Crispy chicken! Biscuits!" He winks. "I'll be back in a few minutes."

I have to let him go. I pull back the curtain just enough. The parking lot is silver. All the cars are silver, like they belong to one company or maybe an army. Kyle stops alongside our car. He gets out his keys, then puts them back in his pocket and walks on. Fast. You can see I have to let him go, just in case he means to ever come back.

ANOTHER MOON

Donald Jacobson frowns at the bathroom door from behind which his wife, Frannie, is splashing in the tub. "My marriage is on the rocks," he says aloud. As though testing a foreign phrase, he repeats, "My marriage is on the rocks," then returns to reading the assigned magazine article, "Behavior Modification: Its Uses in Marriage Counselling." The title is printed over a color photograph of a couple in their late twenties, close to his and Frannie's age. Except that his own hairline is receding in sad, symmetrical ovals, Donald sees a pleasing resemblance between himself and the handsome husband. Both have brown hair, high cheekbones, noses which are so fiercely clipped at the nostrils that several people have told Donald that he looks remarkably like George Hamilton — a compliment which Donald tells Frannie is no compliment at all since George Hamilton is probably a fag and definitely cannot act worth shit, but which Donald secretly cherishes all the same.

The photo-wife with her hairdresser's flip, her executive air, bears no resemblance to Donald's Frannie, who wears her honey blond hair long and loose and hanging to her waist. Donald sees his Frannie as a shy, modern-day Botticelli, an appropriate image since the two first met in their alma mater's darkened screening-room, watching the flashing slides of Renaissance Art 227.

The couple in the photograph stands back to back, each holding a Chinese back-scratcher in one hand and a bull-whip in the other. Donald is reading the article for his night-class in Behavioral Psychology. When he started the course, he laughed, in what he now considers a very immature fashion, at the abbreviation for Behavior Modification. It was scattered throughout the text. "Look, Frannie," he said, and carried his text book into the bathroom. Frannie did not laugh. She wrinkled up her nose and said, in what Donald thought an unnecessarily cruel voice, "I told you it was crap." Her own jokes she thought funny; she was still laughing when he closed the bathroom door behind him.

Donald puts down the magazine and rises from the sofa. He knows what Frannie is doing. She is reading. In the bathtub. Maybe Boswell, maybe *Family Circle* , maybe a textbook on the basic usage of the English language. Lately, whenever Donald wants to find her, he has only to go to the bathroom and knock. Although it is true that their apartment is young-couple small (bath, kitchen, livingroom, bedroom) with no corners to escape to, Donald can't help thinking that there's something neurotic in Frannie spending her evening reading in the tub. Let her do what she likes during the day, he thinks, but at least she can talk to me when I come home from work. (Rolls upon rolls of carpet rise up before him. Cranberry. Avocado. Plush. Shag).

He knocks on the bathroom door. "Frannie?" he asks, nervously, as if uncertain that it is she rocking the tub waters, letting a trickle of hot water keep the bath temperature up.

"Don?" Frannie says. For a moment, Donald feels frightened; Frannie, too, seems to be uncertain as to who is on the other side of the door. Her voice sounds far away. "Don? Did you want something?"

Donald has already thought of an answer to this. He will say nothing about how irritating it is that Frannie is in the tub. He will not reinforce this behavior. He's decided that he can say he needs to floss his teeth. "I need to floss my teeth," he says.

The tub water sloshes and Donald imagines his wife looking towards the door critically, wrinkling up her prettily snubbed nose. "Well," she says with a sigh, "come in."

Donald enters, pulling the door shut behind himself immediately, not allowing the warm air of the bathroom to escape. He heads straight for the medicine cabinet. The mirrored door is steamed over, making it impossible for him to see his reflection. It would seem vain, he knows, if he wiped off the mirror; not wiping it off, however, makes him feel vaguely disturbed. The absence of his reflection from where he expects it always oppresses to Donald; boarded over department store windows have ruined a stroll for him more than once.

He opens the medicine cabinet door and pulls a strand of dental floss from the spool.

"I'm reading *Middlemarch*," Frannie says. She always tells him what she is reading, gives him condensed versions of the books, and, afterwards, asks, "So what do you think of that?"

"I finished *An American Dream* this afternoon." She sits up, resting a fleshy arm on the edge of the tub. Donald thinks she's getting rather fat, has recommended exercise and posted several medically-sound diets on the refrigerator. Floss and fingers sawing at the awkward regions of his mouth, he nods acknowledgement to Frannie's latest book; if he doesn't let her know that he's heard her every word, she might become upset and accuse him of not listening.

"If I thought you'd like the thinking in *that* one," she says, "I'd get a divorce."

Luckily for Donald, he no longer reads. He is proud of his no-nonsense attitude towards his wasted education; he jokes with his co-workers about how valuable four years spent as an English major are when you're working at Carpetland. Anyway, Frannie's threats mean nothing. The year before, she passed through a period in which she put quotations on the bathroom mirror ("Thousands have lived without love, not one without water." W.H. Auden. "If men could get pregnant, abortion would be a sacrament." Flo Kennedy) and carried in her wallet a card from a national women's organization, but it never came to anything; she went no further than writing down on the kitchen calendar the projected dates of their meetings. "You're afraid to go to the grocery alone!" Donald said, scooping her up in his arms and carrying her to the davenport.

"I do what I can in my own way, Donald," she said. "It so happens that I haven't worn make-up for five years, whereas Gloria Steinem streaks her hair. I think that, in my own way, I'm saying as much for The Movement as she is."

"I was only teasing," he said.

"'They also serve who only stand and wait.'"

"I was *just* kidding."

"Hmmm. Well, I really don't believe that, anyway," she said.

"Well, you better believe me," Donald said, feeling slightly piqued. "I said I was kidding."

"No, no, I meant, I don't believe that about 'only standing and waiting.'"

"Okay, because I was kidding."

"Nothing is said in jest, Donald," Frannie said. "Read *The Psycho-pathology of Everyday Life* and weep."

But things are different now, Donald thinks. Actually, things are worse. His wife is becoming fat and secretive and sloppy. He's glad that his mouth is full of floss and fingers. Frannie can't say, "What does that look mean?" But if she should, he can always look innocent and answer, "Just flossing my teeth, Fran."

* * *

He looks up from the text: "When an animal learns to pick a dark gray rather than a light one, using two particular shades of gray, is he responding to the individual shades of gray or to some relationship between them?"

Frannie stands in the doorway, pulling on a pair of pale pink angora mittens. At the fingertips, the mittens are almost mauve. Dirty, Donald thinks. He's told her about the.Woolite twice, but she acts as if she doesn't hear.

"You going somewhere?" he asks.

She studies the back of a mitten and nods. "Dalton's," she says. Her parka has become too small; the zipper puckers from the strain.

But I won't say anything, Donald reminds himself. Everything is cool. A-okay. "I'll be studying," he says, and turns back to his book: "Is the mouse saying 'Pick this one shade?' or 'Pick the darker?'"

After the door closes, Donald looks out the apartment window. He watches Frannie cross the quiet Sunday afternoon street. Dalton's is to the east, but Frannie walks west. He rises from his chair to follow her with his eyes. Her parka hood has an exaggerated ruff of fake-fur; seen from above, his wife seems a huge, exotic, blue flower.

* * *

He waits in a doorway across the street. When Frannie comes down, he follows her. Foremost in his mind is the possibility that his wife is seeing another man; he has time, however, as he trails her down Mount Royal, to consider that unless she loses weight fast, she will never be able to wear shorts

64

this summer.

When she enters the French bakery on Charles, he winces. He watches her though the bakery window. Her long hair, gathered into a chignon at the base of her neck, gives her a bold, peasantish look. She orders two loaves of bread, holding up the middle and index fingers for the shop-girl, then walks toward the park with her package.

By the time she reaches the park, she has made several stops at the small neighborhood shops, purchasing at one a wedge of Brie; at another, a small red box; at another, a pear.

Her thighs take on the bell shape of a carefully untinned *pate de foie gras* when she sits down on the park bench. She tears one of the loaves of bread into small pieces and feeds the pigeons, then begins to eat. No one else comes. She appears to enjoy herself immensely. When she is finished with the second loaf of bread, the cheese and the pear, she removes from the small red box a clever apple of Dutch chocolate which falls into perfect slices when she raps it against the park bench.

* * *

"Frannie," Donald mumbles into her long hair. He rubs her face with his cheek. "Frannie," he says, and slides a hand down the slope of her belly.

"Sleepy, Donald," Frannie says, and rolls over with a great yawn and Buddha stretch. "So sleepy."

* * *

He considers a private-eye. Their bank account is continually overdrawn by checks made out for cash. Where does the money go, Frannie? he asks. Frannie blushes, holds out her pudgy fingers as if illustrating the emptiness of her hands. I try, she says, then laughs a short, nervous laugh, like a guilty child. I try.

* * *

Looking for the car keys, he discovers in her purse one small tin of smoked oysters, three health-food candy bars, and a box of British toffee. He searches the apartment while she is gone; in her winter boots, she stores sheaves of Turkish fruit roll, using the stuff like boot-trees.

There is no one else, Donald tells himself, but he isn't relieved. In the morning, his comb is full of hair. His breath is metallic, he's losing weight. In the past two months, he has missed thirteen days of work while trailing Frannie to a French cafe, to a soul food joint where he witnessed her consumption of double portions of barbecue pork and peach cobbler; there have been trips to a Szechwan kitchen, to the oyster bar in the farmer's market — where Frannie joked with the proprietor who cast ugly looks at the lurking Donald. A narrow escape. The man pointed in Donald's direction, as though asking Frannie if "that fellow over there" had been bothering her. Luckily, Donald had the foresight to plant himself near a vegetable stand; he ducked behind a pile of sweet-corn before Frannie turned his way.

Pastries she eats by the bagful. Spanish food, Mexican, Italian. She spends three minutes selecting a single tangerine from the man who vends fruit out of his pickup truck. Her discrimination seems to please them all. Donald can hardly believe that this woman, testing a wine, debating between Havarti cheeses, is his Frannie. The maitre d' at Marconi's claps his hands at her arrival. The teenagers who work the specialty shops after school forever offer her thin samples of cheese and imported crackers. In one such shop, she holds an olive on her tongue for such a long time — smiling at the girl behind the counter — illustrating her pleasure by rolling her eyes —that Donald enters the shop after she leaves.

"What are those?" He points to the plastic bucket filled with brine and still-bobbling black-green olives.

"Greek olives," says the girl, as she goes on stacking pyramids of Toblerone candies. "2.19 a pound."

"I want one," Donald says.

"They're a nickel a piece," says the girl. She fishes an olive out with a pair of tongs and hands it to Donald. He pops it into his mouth, immediately spits it out.

"It tastes like motor oil!" he cries indignantly. The girl begins to laugh, but she stops when Donald presses the chewed fruit into her hand and storms out the door.

* * *

Frannie clears the dinner plates and carries them to the sink. Donald balances on the back two legs of his chair, feeling a manic cheerfulness, like a boy who runs whooping along the edges of the pool, certain that being in the water will be wonderful, but unable to get up the nerve to jump in.

"It dents the linoleum when you do that, Don," Frannie says as she removes the glasses from the table.

"Right, right," Donald says, and sets all four legs of the chair on the floor. "Hey, listen, Frannie, I wanted to tell you I'm really proud of the way you only ate one pork chop and left the peas on your plate."

"What?" she says as she rinses the glasses out under the tap. "What did you say?" She shuts off the water and turns around.

"I said, you know, I thought that was good, the way you left your peas and only ate one pork chop."

She tilts her head to one side, a little frown on her forehead. She runs her tongue over her teeth, back and forth, several times, then breaks into a smile. "I know what it is," she says. "I know *exactly*. I don't like pork chops and peas, Donald. Not at all."

* * *

66

Donald looks out the class-room window. He waits for the instructor to answer his question. His face is warm and there's a song he particularly hates running through his head. "Star-crossed lo-o-overs . . ." It's one of several hits from out of Donald's past in which the lover-singer asks Father Sebastian or some such figure for advice, pretending the advice is for "a friend."

All of the other students have left. The instructor fastens his motorcycle helmet under his chin. Donald wonders if the instructor is younger than himself; if so, he hopes the instructor doesn't know that that's the case.

The instructor slips on a leather jacket, goggles, and gloves. Donald senses that the man is suddenly transformed, potentially dangerous. The man punches Donald in the arm and smiles, but the force of the blow is far from comradely.

"You want to eliminate a behavior, ignore it," he says. "You ought to know that by now, man."

* * *

Parts of Frannie's body are not covered by the bath water. Her belly is a soft white island with breasts and knees as coral reefs. She lies flat in the tub, ears submerged, holding in her hands a soggy copy of the magazine which contains the article, "Behavior Modification: Its Uses in Marriage Counselling."

Donald steps closer to her, her flesh looks too red. He bends over, sticks a finger in the water.

"Frannie!"

She looks up at him dumbly. Her hair fans out around her face in silvery blond streams. "What?" she says, without lifting her head out of the water.

"It's way too hot!"

Frannie sits up in the tub. Half of her face is white, half is red. Her nipples are surrounded by a concentric band of pale flesh above scarlet. "What did you say?" she asks calmly, her face abstracted. "I couldn't hear you."

"It's too hot!"

She holds the wet magazine out to him. "You can take this," she says and slides back into the water. "It's totally lacking in imagination."

* * *

Donald sits in his blue Chevy, the engine idling. He looks across the street to the cafe window with the gold letters: Icarus. He turns off the car and gets out. Short, handsome Greek men lean against the building. Donald envies them their mustaches, their wiry hair. Probably, they're sailors, he thinks; he hopes, as he puts his own back to the building wall, that they won't think he's gay.

The last time that he followed Frannie here, he spied her at a table underneath a painting, a boy falling from the sky — one bare leg crashing towards the ocean. He watched her expertly stick the tines of her fork into a wedge of lemon and dress a plate of what seemed to be steamed greens with the fruit's juices. The action, so sure, so deft, left him feeling slightly sick with love.

He sidles up to the window and peeks in. There she is, eating the little crispy things that remind Donald of canned onion rings — yes, fried baby eels. Frannie dabs at her mouth with a linen napkin. As though no one will notice how much she eats, Donald thinks. He's noticed that the fatter she gets, the more mannerly she becomes at the table. At home, she eats slow-slow, poising her fork in front of her mouth, like Snow White instructing the Disney dwarves in table-manners. One-two-three-four. she does a little dance of gestures with her utensils. The tilt of her arms as she slices a corner off a steak or a pork chop makes Donald think of hunters' photographs: a duck taking off from water.

She signals to the waiter. The man comes to her smiling. She speaks to him, her face composed along the lines of a Rafael Madonna. The waiter has a romantically ratty look to him. Could there be something there? No. The waiter removes her plate with the air of a satisfied retainer, leaving Frannie sipping from a heavy, white coffee cup.

Donald has been here with her in the past, but now he is afraid to return. He worries that someone will say to her — something like — "The usual?" And then what would he do? And she, would she act as if the person were mistaken? Or would she say, "Yes, the usual," as though there were nothing awkward about the situation?

The waiter comes back with a small plate. Baklava. Frannie looks up at him graciously. Such aplomb, Donald thinks. In restaurants, she is graceful, with a power beyond her early "Primavera." She bites into the layered dessert. A bright bit of honeyed filo sparkles on her nether lip like mica. She draws it in with her tongue. Between bites, she folds her hands on the linen table cloth and smiles at the white walls, the waiters, the other patrons.

* * *

She stands in the doorway, hands on enormous hips, wearing a suit of soft gray wool. Donald doesn't know where or when she got the suit, but expects an overdraft call from the bank soon. The suit is obviously an expensive one, so expensive, in fact, that it frightens Donald. Why would she spend so much on a suit, matching gloves, boots, accessories, unless she planned on not getting smaller again?

"Is that it?" asks the man from The Salvation Army. He has in his arms a last box of clothes. Donald does not look up from the selection on "Perception: Behavioral Input," does not acknowledge the presence of the man from Salvation Army, who has carried out the six boxes filled with Frannie's too small t-shirts, shorts, jeans, and more.

Donald reads for perhaps the sixth time in the last half-hour:

> If a spot moves toward another at a certain speed, and the other moves
> away at a certain time and at a certain speed, causation of the second

movement by the first is reported, even if the two do not quite touch one another. The effect is effortlessly "perceived" and seems in no way like an "inference" or a "conclusion."

"Good-bye," Frannie calls down the stairs after the Salvation Army man. "Thank you."

She walks by Donald, the floor creaks with her weight. He sees how she fills the hallway to the kitchen with her broad back, moves between the narrow walls like a ship in a lock. "Stop!" he almost cries out; her head seems about to hit the globe lamp which hangs from the ceiling; but, no, she passes into the kitchen unharmed.

He waits for the manic hum of the open refrigerator to begin. A cupboard door opens and closes. There is a sound of chopping. He pushes back his chair, quietly, quietly, and walks down the hall.

Above him, the globe lamp is white, a gigantic pearl, an accessible moon. He must reach high, arm fully extended, in order to touch its cool surface.

* * *

He abandons the woman in red who can't decide between tweed or olive shag. He crosses the showroom and presses a sheet of notebook paper into the manager's hand. The manager turns and frowns. "What's this, Don?" he asks.

"Look. Larry, I've got to get out of here. Those are the dimensions for that lady's rec-room." Donald points towards the store's economy section. The woman in red, looking sad and alone, disappears behind several rolls of royal blue carpeting.

"You leave now, buddy, and you're through," the manager hisses. Don is trying to unpin his name tag; he looks up at the manager in surprise. "I mean it, Don," the manager says.

"It's an emergency," Donald says, "You'd understand," and rushes out the back entrance.

* * *

He calls from a phone booth near the apartment.

"Hello," Frannie says. "Hello? Hello?" Donald walks to the alley across from the apartment and waits for her to leave.

* * *

Strawberries, whipped cream, meringue. Four layers. Donald counts them as the waiter lifts the entire torte off the serving-cart and sets it in front of Frannie. She is bathed in the restaurant's soft pink lights and seated on a chair covered with wine-colored velvet. Her hair is piled on top of her head in elaborate swirls. The year before, she was t-shirts and blue-jeans; today, in pale blue silk, she looks like the wife of a German ambassador.

The chef joins the waiter at her elbow. Frannie says something that makes them smile. She squeezes the chef's hand and gestures toward the torte. An invitation to make the first cut? Donald wonders. Rain blows under the restaurant's canvas awning. He shivers.

Beneath the chef's expert hand, the meringue gives way. The waiter piles a wobbling portion onto a serving plate and sets it before Frannie. She takes a bite. They wait for her reaction. She approves, half-jokingly offers the chef a bite of torte off her fork. Donald feels as if he is watching a movie shot with a vaselined-lens. The camera is on Frannie, who sends her smiles out to the people around her.

It is too much. Donald rushes into the restaurant, knocking over the placard that lists the menu of the day. The people turn their eyes away from Frannie and peer at Donald. In the moment of quiet that follows, his fingers running through the fronds of a potted palm in the foyer, Donald believes that Frannie will blush, will rise from her chair in confusion; instead, she reaches for her glass of chablis like a woman steadying herself at a railing. She takes a sip, dabs at her pink, pursed lips with a napkin. By the time she sinks her fork back into the next section of the torte, she is able to look at him without a sign of recognition.

"May we help you, sir?" asks the maitre d'.

Donald does not answer. He backs out the door and into the rain. He walks around to the other side of the restaurant and peers through the window. He cannot see the whole of Frannie, only her heavy arm, her hand, the triumphant clearing away of whipped cream and meringue and strawberries.

He is afraid to go, afraid to stay. He raps on the window with his knuckles, but no one at all looks up from the pleasure of their meal.

BLUE NEWS

I coiled the phone cord about myself, around and around, and made faces for Rand. He didn't look up. He was chipping away at the kitchen tile we had hated through four years of marriage and finally decided we could no longer bear. Tcht, tcht, tcht, hammer against chisel, and all was well, baby asleep, cheek all lovely pudding on the joyful bells and bunnies of his playpen pad.

Into my ear, my sister said, "Manny wants me to make him something with plantains! His mother cooks with plantains! He's got this picture of his family, in front of their apartment building — " Here Betsy's voice clotted with emotion. "His grandma's in the picture, this little tiny thing. She knew Papa Doc or somebody — Trujillo? — somebody like that once."

"Hm," I said while Betsy cleared her throat. I had yet to meet this maker of dreams, Manny, but Betsy's response to him was no surprise. She had fallen for the Hebrew traditions of her ex-husband Dino's family wth the same ardour: oh, matzohs! oh, Passover! oh, grandmother escaping from Russia! Perhaps our French-Welsh-Scotch-Irish-German-English-Dutch background was too diffuse for Betsy and she needed to get under somebody else's yarmulke, sombrero, beret?

I hadn't minded all the hubub over Dino because Dino was nice, but as a rule Betsy chose men because they had a shimmer to them — like bad meat and the backs of flies.

"He's the coolest guy in town," she said, jejune as a junior high girl. "He's sly, like a fox. He's got friends on the police force."

"Great," I said, making my voice dull. "Just great."

Betsy laughed. "Well, it's true. And he's so gorgeous." Her voice tripped into a hole of anger to cry: "All these little bitches follow him around, you wouldn't believe it!" But then she laughed again. "It's a real fight for the mirror at our house!"

Rand sat back on his haunches, a little pearl of sweat clinging to the tip of his nose. I put my hand to my forehead to give him some idea of what poured into my ear. But I didn't want the conversation to end. I missed Betsy. Back in the days of Dino, she and I sat in her kitchen for hours, talking, laughing, sometimes saying whole sentences in stereo; the two of us being married at the same time was good as summers at the cottage, when she had to play with me, or play alone.

"Listen," Betsy said abruptly, "I've got to go."

"Oh. Okay," I said.

"Tell Rand 'hello.'"

I uncoiled myself from the phone cord. A chair fitted itself under my bottom. I sank my head into my palms, drilled elbows into thighs. Betsy, Betsy.

Tcht, tcht. When Rand was doing the chipping, pleasing platelets of old tile flipping off his chisel like tiddlywinks, I wished I were chipping along side of him. Which was funny because I'd done half the floor the weekend before and hated the job.

I got up and gathered the tile chips he'd piled to one side and placed them on top of a too-full sack of garbage. Would they fall, would they stay? The talk with Betsy made me feel the responsible citizen; I summoned up the energy to shake out an empty grocery bag and place it next to the overflowing one.

"Rand," I said, my voice all full of sighs and troubles, "what are we going to do?"

He shrugged. "Maybe you shouldn't talk to her, it upsets you so much."

"She's my sister!"

Rand, being an only child, could hardly understand such logic. "What's for dinner?" he said.

"Rand! My sister!" I was worried. The *best* news Betsy delivered in her increasingly rare phone calls was that Manny had a "terrific body": his muscles were so hard, she said with nothing short of glee, that it was not even comfortable to sleep with her head on his shoulder, but she did, of course, she did. The other news, which arrived on sadder days, was that the University didn't want Manny to play basketball; that Manny was a dealer; that he didn't always come back to the apartment at night; that he carried a gun.

I'd *told* Rand all of this. We talked it over and over. But here he was, unruffled as one of those lakes, painted, underglass, in a natural history museum. Rand socked me in the ear once, on a rare occasion when we were both drunk on sangria; he looked at me in confusion as I lay curled in the corner of the bathroom, later swore he hadn't even done it; but generally, he was responsible, dependable. He did the books for an aluminum plant in the same town where I taught history. He was okay with the baby. He never went out at night and left me home alone. We'd met at college, where, on our first date, we went to a ceramics exhibit and shared a blueberry doughnut.

Manny and Betsy's first date took place in his then girlfriend's car. "Obviously, he doesn't like *her*!," Betsy had told me in a dopey, triumphant, love-stricken voice.

"Mm," I said.

We are attractive women, my sister and I; even with our long faces and wide hips there have always been men willing to call us beautiful. Our parents may have set us worrying when they compared us so unfavorably to The Lennon Sisters, but once we escaped the electronically-grayed Saturday nights and moved out onto the slick tiled edges of swimming pools, the blond dance floors, more than enough boys tabulated our virtues; sometimes the arms ached from the very act of resistance. I could not explain Betsy's being enamoured with Manny in terms of desperation. I couldn't explain it at all.

Though people often said I seemed the older of the two of us, *I* could remember the facts: me courting her, imitating her, even throwing money to her out of my bedroom door when she threatened to kill me unless I told her how much Mother had spent on my Christmas doll. I could remember, still later, her throwing the doll at me, hitting my temple hard — the only time in my life I saw stars, felty stars of turquoise and umbrous purple. "Stop blubbering!" she had commanded, borrowing the word from our father. "I can't stand blubbering!"

For me, she was still my older sister. She was supposed to have some wisdom I did not, and if she didn't, I needed to see how she had missed it, if she had given it up for something else. The first chance I got, I went to visit.

Down our gravel road I drove, backwards, because there was no turnabout. The lilacs opened on either side, making me thankful for air, nose, the damp of the gravel and the sun's warmth. The lilacs surprised me; they didn't seem to go with the gruff farmer who rented to us; but perhaps he was different back in the days of their planting. "Slicker than a mole's back," he'd told us when we moved in, "that's how I want this lawn kept."

I gave myself a pep talk as I drove the country roads. Maybe he'd be okay. Maybe she'd turn his head around. He'd turn her head around. She'd get bored. She'd just had bad luck. Fallen for more creeps than most, but, hell, everyone loved a creep or two, *I* loved a creep once — though I always kept myself covered with a nice boy on the side.

The stop sign at the end of the road signalled the beginning of the highway — smooth, silent sailing all the way to the city, where the street lights opened their green eyes to me, pulled me forward so fast I almost missed the turn-off. But there it was. And a few blocks later, the squat duplex, gray with several of its roof shingles standing up like cowlicks.

A dark, skinny boy balancing on Swedish clogs answered the door. "'Ello" he said, retreating into a dark room, its floor rattling with newspapers. A scruffy little dog rushed at me and began to bark. "Quiet, there," the boy said, and pushed the dog back into the room.

"You must be Manny," I said, shocked by what a kid he was. Betsy was twenty-eight. *I* taught history to senior high boys who looked older than Manny. But then Betsy entered the room, scolding the dog, a charming blush spreading over her face.

She was wonderfully skinny and, with the color high in her cheeks, her wild air, she reminded me of one of Dostoevsky's grand consumptives. I immediately wished myself twenty pounds thinner, out of my classroom clothes and into a khaki jumpsuit like Betsy wore. The tobacco-smell of dog piss was small consolation.

Betsy flapped her arms like some great bird. "Oh!" she said, and put Michael Jackson on the turntable, but, really, she bet I'd rather hear Marvin Gaye singing "After the Dance."

"Oh, yes!" I said. Marvin Gaye always made me weak with pleasure, Marvin Gaye singing somewhere up in the stars, being so good and strong and beautiful.

"Marvin Gaye. That old man," Manny said, but he smiled and gave Betsy a hug which made me sigh in relief. Thank you, thank you. Betsy leaned into him, as if she were a sleepy, happy kid. "Listen, we were just going to do a little coke," she said, and held out half a Happy Clown straw.

"Nah, I'll just look at this, or something," I said. I picked up a fashion magazine; several pages stuck to the floor. The top one declared, "I went from a 34A to a 36C!"

Betsy giggled. "The dog's not trained yet. This place usually looks better, Jane, honest."

"Yeah, sure," Manny said and, grinning, he edged her into the kitchen.

I read an article on the eyebrow grooming decisions of Lauren Hutton, Cher, and others. Sophia Loren, it turned out, swept her brows up, snipped them short with a pair of manicure scissors, and then glued them into place.

"How you doing, Jane?" Betsy called from the kitchen; it seemed she and Manny were arguing about something.

"I'm okay," I said. I reached down to pet the puppy. It skittered through the newspapers. It came back, sniffed with its cold nose. The paws came up and scrabbled at my knees. "You're a little wild, aren't you?" I said. I meant to sound jocular, but when it nipped at my hands, its teeth were sharp; my efforts at soothing the animal seemed to stir it up, if anything.

I escaped into the bathroom, toeing the dog away from the door. I inspected my eyebrows. Some of the hairs dropped, and I plucked them out with a pair of tweezers found on an admirably crusty shelf.

"What the fuck is she calling here for?" Betsy said on the other side of the door.

"Be cool," Manny said, "we got your sister here, man."

Betsy imitated a breathy-voiced woman: "Ahh, is Manuel there? Oh, no, no, no, no, no, I don't need to leave a message. I'll be talking to him later."

"She don't know what she be talking about," Manny said.

Betsy's voice rose in pitch, the note of despair I remembered only in connection with lovers, a song for men: "It's the one you had the picture of when you came back from Chicago, isn't it? Isn't it?"

"You dreaming, man," said Manny. And then he was gone. Betsy knocked on the bathroom door. "He's got to play ball and do a little business. He be back later."

He be back?

She pulled a pan from a cardboard box on the floor and began assembling a Brunswick stew. Despite the room's disorder, she did not throw all the things together, but cooked, separately, the chicken, the lima beans, and so on. I never ate anything she made that wasn't wonderful. "Hey." She rattled a little bag in front of my face.

"Candy corn! I haven't eaten candy corn in a million years!"

"I want you to look at something," she said. And disappeared into the bedroom. She returned with a piece of paper and an envelope. Lilac scented lilac. "What's this say?"

I shifted my feet beneath the table. Brown and white and crazy, that dog settled down to the destruction of my shoe laces.

The letter was in Spanish, which I hadn't studied since a chubby man on tv asked my tenth grade class, "¿Que hay en el pozo?" But I did my best for Betsy. As far as I could tell, the letter was the sort one wrote when in love but trying to appear only enticingly friendly.

"'Cousin,' she signs herself, 'your little cousin.'"

"Oh, you're kidding! It's from his *cousin*."

"Hold on," I said, and read the note again. "I don't know, see, I can't tell how intense this is. Cousin may be one of those ironic things. I think it's used pretty widely."

Betsy shrugged, took the letter from me, stuffed it in her pocket. "I don't suppose he'll want this," she said, peering into the final mixture on the stove.

"Why don't we eat?" It was already nine. Out in the country — so far away, it seemed — Rand and Danny would have eaten at six; my stomach was beginning to growl.

Betsy walked to the window and looked out. "You go ahead," she said. She seemed a little sad. To cheer her up, I mashed a couple candy corn on my teeth, just like we had as kids, transforming our mouths into terrible carbuncles.

"Where are the bowls?" I said, holding my lips wide so she couldn't miss the mess on my teeth.

She turned from the window. "Oh!" She laughed, opened a cupboard for me. Inside was a single blue bowl, a cardboard shoe box of utensils, a dusty jar of grape leaves. "When we first brought the dog home, I gave it some scraps in one of these bowls," Betsy said. "Manny picked it up and he, like, *threw* it into the sink! I don't think he'd ever eaten on china before, he was sort of shocked when it broke!"

I took the bowl from the cupboard. Her "everydays" from the marriage to Dino. How I'd admired those dishes when she lifted them from their tissue-lined boxes! Though each bowl had been a cobalt blue, there were four different patterns for the plates: one, a tattersall of blue lines on a white ground; one, white squiggles on a blue ground; one, overall blue flowers fierce as thunderheads; and one, tidy checks of blue and white. At the time, I had wished I were just getting married; Rand and my brown Dansk seemed suddenly stodgy. I wanted to remove myself with a wild mix of yellow mugs and fire engine red plates. Birds of Paradise on black porcelain were not too lush for me. But, now, as I stood in Betsy's kitchen, I reached the happy conclusion that all that cobalt and white had been a little —faddy. My dishes were, as they say, available in fine stores everywhere, cleverly teamed with nubby napkins and handsome tumblers, placecards indicating what lucky couple wanted you to buy this saucer, this knife, that placemat. What we broke, we could replace.

I sat down with my bowl of stew. Betsy set about razoring another line of cocaine. "Manny's lousy at business," she said, her forehead knotted in concentration. "He doesn't know *how* bad. You know those stock checks we got around Christmas?"

I nodded.

"He blew all *that* — and now we've got people owing us, like, seventy-five hundred. He just goes out and does lines with the customers." She ran a moistened finger across the formica-topped table, rubbed the finger across her gums. "He thinks people would rather deal with him because he's good at it! It's because *I* expect them to pay. *I* take care of business."

She went back to looking out the window.

"So what's up with you, Jane? You guys have your garden in yet? I wish we had a garden."

Manny returned at about ten-thirty. "Man," he said, "I been playing ball, I need some *meat*."

"That stew's wonderful," I said.

Manny smiled, put his Yankee's cap on Betsy's head. "Let's go over that Sirloin Stockade," he said.

Betsy rolled her eyes, but she put on her coat, asked: How was his game? Did he see Spoon? Did Mickey pay?

Outside, it had started to drizzle, just a light spring thing which made the air something to pay attention to. I climbed into the back of the car, behind the horizon of Manny and Betsy. Manny clicked a tape in and we were off.

The place turned out to be a kind of steak cafeteria. I nudged Betsy as we went in and she giggled; the inside looked like a basement rec room converted into a drive-in: barnboard, backlit photos of frilly salads and tinfoiled baked potatoes.

When Manny cut into his steak, I noticed the muscle in his arm contracted to a gorgeous apple — not some weight lifter's striated piece of glossy meat, but a healthy apple of muscle — something to rejoice in for its simple rightness.

Was that what this was all about?

Manny speared a sheaf of iceburg lettuce coated with Thousand Island, said, "I figure, I get the degree, then — it's like I go on a trip, I always pack more than I going to need."

He referred to his college studies in Recreation, how they might come in handy if he couldn't get a pro ball contract. He looked at me, as if for a response. I nodded dumbly, embarrassed for all three of us. I knew Betsy wrote all his papers and take-home exams and that he had not been to class more than twice all semester. He wasn't stupid — anybody who could get around Betsy couldn't be — so I figured we all knew there wasn't going to be a pro contract, a sailing away to that rarified world of camera-lit courts and endorsements for beer.

A damp discomfort settled. Betsy and I sipped at our iced teas. I referred to one of my students as egom*a*niacal and Betsy crisply corrected my pronunciation. "Isn't it egoman*i*acal?" she asked, and I said I guessed she was right.

Later, when the mood had lifted, and she put me, laughing, into my car, she whispered, "We're so much alike, you see?"

I thrilled, briefly, at the words, then realized she meant Manny and herself. An equation stamped its way across my head. I am to Betsy as Betsy is to

Manny. Or, Betsy is to me as Manny is to Betsy?

Pale moons of farmhouses rose out of their woodlots every few miles on the road home. Our shimmering gravel drive seemed to climb skyward to the big white shape floating at its end. As soon as I got out of the car, I called up to the dark bedroom window, "Rand, I'm home!" although I knew he was asleep and would not wake.

* * *

Betsy phoned a few weeks later, catching me on the way to work. "This dog is *never* going to get housebroken, and Manny's having a fit! Ooo, I think it's going to turn out ugly, too, now it's not such a puppy."

"You ought to try that cage method," I told her. "You just get a box and you —"

"Manny tried to strangle me!" she wailed. "He's crazy! He hit me with the lamp and then he started strangling me with the cord. I was blacking out. Then he started in on the dog!"

I kicked the woodwork with the toe of my shoe. "You get out of there!" I said, crying, but mad, mad, even a little exhilarated. I felt closer to her than I had since those days before she divorced Dino, and she and I sat in their kitchen, drinking coffee from the blue cups, laughing, switching to chablis as the sun began its woozy decline and we started work on a fine feast for Dino and Rand.

"You get out of there, now, please! I'll drive in and get you. You can stay out here as long as you like."

She inhaled. "Just a minute," she said, then, "Listen, I'll call you back later, Jane, okay?"

I confess that, in spite of my agitation, it occurred to me that having her at the house would be fun. I put striped sheets on the spare bed in the baby's room before I left for work. I stopped at the liquor store near Danny's daycare and bought a bottle of wine. I stuck it between the milk and apples in the refrigerator when Danny and I got home, then I dialed Betsy's number.

She was distant. She said she was busy. She hung up.

I drank the bottle of chablis, quite warm, except for the glass I judiciously reserved for Rand before starting in. When he got home, I told him, in my blubbery way, blubbering into the baby's feathery hair, how Betsy was in danger.

He shook his head. "Betsy, Betsy." He went to clean up for dinner. Danny, bored, shoved his feet against my chest. I clamped him into his high chair and fed him smelly spoonfuls of strained chicken.

* * *

"You have to consider it a bad sign when a guy steals his girl's car to take you out on your first date," I said, not to Betsy, but to Rand, who was watching Angie Dickinson and Earl Holliman discuss the best way to stop

77

crime in Los Estados Unidos while simultaneously allowing Angie to reveal and endanger her incredibly well-maintained figure.

"Don't tell me," Rand said. "I wouldn't marry him for a million dollars." He smiled without taking his eyes from the television.

"My God, you don't suppose she'd marry him, do you?"

"Of course she will."

Rand turned away from the set. I was pleased. Some attention? Hello, hello? He made a little face, rubbed his fingers together as people often do when talking money, then he was gone again, lost in images. Rand did not know that I had recently borrowed five hundred dollars from my father and mother in order to loan it to Betsy, or that I had pretended to believe the money went to repair the brake shoes on her car. He did not know that I had in my jewelry box a recipe for a love potion. I'd copied it down on a deposit slip one sunny day while driving home from work. A benign offering from a witch interviewed on NPR. "You can marinate a steak in it," this very up to date witch said, "or put it in a casserole." Rosemary was the only ingredient which my extensive spice cabinet did not contain. I considered the red and white cans of the stuff while shopping for dill or basil or mustard seed, but I never bought rosemary. I was afraid to barbecue a love-potioned chicken and feed it to Rand. I figured that if it worked, and, afterwards, Rand loved me more, I'd always wonder: is this mine, or the potion's? I never thought to take it myself. I saw my love as some ineluctable fixture — The Statue of Liberty, Arc de Triomphe, The Pyramids at Gyzeh — waiting to greet him when he finally decided to turn my way.

* * *

I shopped in the city quite a bit that summer, showed up at Manny and Betsy's unannounced. If we were alone, the news was always bad: more phone calls, threats, the dog returned to the pound. Manny convinced her to quit her job; then he drove off in her car, left her stranded in that cardboard box-filled apartment.

The first time I saw him with another woman was in front of the A&P, and it might as well have been Rand from the sickness I felt. Dear Abby be damned, I called Betsy from the neighboring gas station while my groceries bred bacteria in the Pinto.

"I'll look into this," Betsy said cooly, as if I had just given her a report on one of her employees. She hung up.

A few hours later, she called my house. "That was just Celeste," she said, laughing. "She's an old friend."

"She looked pretty new to me," I said. "About ten years newer than you or me."

"Yes, yes," Betsy said, "She's like a little sister to him, you know, she wants advice about boys and things."

I felt betrayed. It occurred to me that in one of those lifeboat situations, I would save her before Rand, but that I'd be going down, lungs filled with water, while she hoisted Manny over the gunwales. I saw a flotilla of lifeboats, swimmers amidst the jetsam, some taking command of a boat, tossing out a passenger, then diving in for a victim; the rescued diving after someone else. Things were very busy, and wet.

Manny began to stay away days at a time. "I lie on the couch waiting," she said, her voice cracking with sadness and fatigue. "I'm a good person. I would *never* do anything with another man, but he accuses me. I'm walking from the bathroom to the bedroom in my robe and some of his friends are over, so he says, really loud, 'You think anybody here wants to see your tits, you crazy.'" She started blubbering and I patted her on the back.

Manny was in the bedroom then and she spoke loud enough that I knew she hoped he would hear. He spent most of his time in the bedroom as far as I could tell. He liked to watch TV with the sound off, stereo on.

She took me into the bedroom to say hello. "Hey, Jane!" Manny said, "What's happening?" Very nice. A cute hat on his head, bedsheet halfway up his corrugated middle. He was watching *Password*; I wondered what pleasure there could be in the game without the sound.

I dragged her away from the place for a minute, hoping to get a cheese sandwich or something into her hollow cheeks. I said, "Why like a guy like that?"

"I know, I know." Then her face brightened. "Spoon and Denby and Grover were all at the apartment last night and you would not have believed — they started doing this music thing, slapping and clapping! Denby's from Jamaica, you know, I told you about Denby, he's so cute, this really little guy, and they're all playing on their bodies. The sounds they made! I couldn't believe it."

What could I say? She was a *turista*. She was visiting a foreign land, entranced by the breezes. She stopped calling, except in the worst of times:

"I got Jenny to drive me out there. I had a feeling. I said to this chambermaid — I'd met her before when we were doing some deals out there — 'Uh, miss, I was wondering if you could let me into my motel room because my husband's asleep in there and I don't want to wake him up.' She was happy to help out, no problem, right this way. Boy, was he surprised to see me!" Her voice was wobbly, but triumphant.

"Well?" I asked.

She sighed into the phone. "There was somebody with him. She was in bed, but, even *she* said they hadn't been doing anything, so I don't know. But I was cool. He was dressed, see? If he hadn't been dressed, I might have lost it, but she kept saying they hadn't been doing anything."

"Oh, Betsy, come on!" The last time she had called me he was threatening to kill her — not just at that moment, but on a regular basis. "Why do you tell me these things?" I had cried. "If anything happens to you, I'll tell them everything, every little thing I know. Let Manny know that, Betsy, that I know plenty of stuff!"

"I wouldn't want him to go to jail," she said, "No, Jane, I'd rather he had to suffer the guilt, knowing what he'd done."

When I gave Rand the motel story, he said, "This is all we talk about anymore, do you know that, Jane?"

I was cleaning mashed Cheerios out of the seams of Danny's highchair just then, so I didn't have to meet Rand's eyes right away. I supposed what he said was true. We talked about lots of other things, of course, but Manny and Betsy were the topic I found most interesting.

"I know it makes you sad. It's a sad story," he said, "but I think you're going to have to stop letting her give it to you. And you've got to stop wanting it."

I wandered into the bedroom and lay face down on the carpet, my nose in the dust and fluff of our days. I once read somewhere that millions of arachnids live in the rugs and mattresses of the world, eating up the miniscule flakes of skin we leave behind. I sneezed and then, as if the sneeze were permission, I began to cry.

Danny, eager as a puppy, galloped into the room on his squeaking corduroy knees. Rand and I could never decide whether to give him a sibling; we never got beyond agreeing we could welcome an accident.

A brother, a sister.

I thought about what Rand had said about Betsy. What if she *were* happy, I thought, wouldn't I be happy if she were happy?

I rose up on my knees and elbows and rubbed my cheek along Dan's. He fell over, laughing. "Well!" I said, and butted my head into his stomach so he would laugh some more. Then I got out the vacuum and swept the carpet with long, loving strokes, this way and that, making stripes of dark or pale blue, depending upon whether I pulled or pushed. Just the way Betsy and I used to make tracks in our mother's beaver coat when we were church girls and sat, one on either side of her, separated against quarrels and laughter, while the minister raised his draped arms towards the ceiling and directed us all to love one another.

DESERT BIRDS

It was on Etter's fifty-seventh birthday that Jack died. Leaning over to help her blow out the birthday candles, his heart simply gave up. As he fell forward, one of the candles caught fire to his hair, a handsome silvery harvest he'd let grow a bit after the heyday of hippies and freaks; Etter swatted out the flames with her hands.

"You'll be better off down here," the children said, referring to the Tucson condominium she and Jack had purchased two years before. She knew her moving there would make the children feel they did something —without their actually having to expend any effort. They both lived in Tucson, young people in a land of retirement.

She tilted a hair forward in her midrow seat as the plane lifted away from Minnesota's lucent beans and boomerangs of blue, as cars and cows shrank to the plastic playthings she'd bought Peter when he was a boy. The cows became raisins, they disappeared. She smiled politely at the woman in the window seat, as if the woman had made a gift of the view, and the woman nodded.

Well. Etter slipped her hand between the seat belt and her waist, checking the clasp. She did not have to sell the big house on White Bear, or say goodbye to the clear, snail-bottomed lake. She did not have to do anything, the lawyers said, just sit tight, see how things went. She wanted to see her grandchildren. She wanted to be near her own children, though sometimes that desire seemed a mixing of her own life with someone else's. Once, Jack said that the only thing the children ever did was come between himself and Etter; she had cried then and not just for the harshness of his words, but for the ache which must have prompted them.

After the funeral, on the phone, in letters, Peter and Lenny kept asking, "What are you going to do now, Mother?" Presumptuous, suddenly bossy. As if she could no longer do what she had done for the last thirty-six years. There seemed to be some truth in this. During the wretched weeks after the funeral, solitary save the occasional lawyer looking over papers in Jack's office, she had found herself frightened by certain noises. It was then that she arranged for people to check the heating and plumbing, then that she made her plane reservations.

She still owned an image of herself and Jack futuring in Arizona. They sat in their courtyard, her just-washed hair grown long, drying in the sun before she twisted it into a simple bun. They watched the boat-tailed grackles feed on the patio, the Gambel's Quail — harem-jewel hanging over the eye — roost along the oleander wall. They picked a topic — Indian crafts, desert fauna, birds — and read up on it together.

She smiled as she took a plastic tumbler of 7-Up from the flight attendant. His eyes were very large and his skin caramel-colored. Perhaps he was an Indian — an India Indian. "Can I get you a pillow?" he asked.

"No, thank you." She titled her head back, shook it, demonstrating her neck was fine. He reminded her a little of her father in the sepia pictures taken before she was born. Hair smooth and dark and a little old-fashioned. When he reached over the aisle passenger to give Etter her bag of barbecued almonds, she blurted, "You certainly have beautiful hands!" The compliment made her weak. Her eyes began to tear — how silly! — but he simply edged his cart to the next row. The woman by the window patted Etter on the arm, and Etter turned towards her, grateful. "I don't think he heard you, dear," the woman whispered. "They *were* lovely, weren't they?" She was an Aussie, she said. The United States were quite a disappointment to her, and here's why.

Jack, Etter thought, would have managed to change the subject. As it was, she listened to the woman until Denver, then flew on to Tucson next to a young, absorbed businessman. She tried to read from the glossy book on Kachina dolls which her daughter, Lenny, had sent — very nice of Lenny — but a part of Etter was on the prowl for some pleasant thing to say to the young man, almost as if to prove to herself she wasn't like the woman on the other flight. When had this trip taken on such a therapeutic quality? She thought of friends who'd flown away for extravagant weeks at La Costa or The Golden Door, returning smooth and brown as hand-dipped chocolates. She mustn't lie. She was no different from most. All her life she'd wanted to be a magical somebody else who was still herself.

The young man seated next to her smiled when she passed him his creamer packets, then he went back to reading from a notebook notched by plastic index tabs, bright as stained glass over printed titles: CHARTING GROWTH, SALES TECHNIQUES, MEETING THE PUBLIC.

* * *

Peter and his Katie and Rob were waiting for her at the airport. She knelt to the grandchildren and they hugged her, rocked her back on her high heels; Peter had to steady her shoulder with his hand. When she looked up to smile, she found his lips trembling. They crushed into each others arms for a moment, confusing the grandchildren, who tugged at grown-up knees for attention.

"Well, it's lucky I have a hand for each, isn't it, Peter?" she said as she and her son backed out of the embrace.

It was a shame, she thought, as he went on ahead for the luggage, his letting himself get so heavy. Though lacking Jack's charm, Peter was a handsome man. Only thirty-four. Or already thirty-four. He should think about his heart. But it was too soon after Jack to say anything about that. Jack was fat once, after the War. After the War, everyone was fat. In old photos, she and her friends shot their Great Plains thighs towards vacation-time cameras without shame. Jack's cleft chin appeared positively incised.

She'd lost twenty-seven pounds since he died: the same twenty-seven pounds she'd been trying to lose ever since Lenny was born. Peter could not have missed the change; perhaps he thought he shouldn't mention it. She was sad and a little proud when Katie asked, "Are you our same grandma?" and insisted Etter sit in the back seat with them.

In Minnesota, she was moving into fall; here the car had the hot-vinyl smell of summer. There were palm trees, mountains. Even now, after years of traveling with Jack, such scenes still had a foreign tang, like a set for a TV detective show. She leaned forward, watching, as Peter moved in and out of the lanes of traffic. Jack had always done their driving here. While packing she'd looked at a map of the city and panicked; she could not even find their street. "Your street isn't on the map yet," said Lenny, long distance. "Too new."

An ambulance clamored by and the children shrieked with pleasure. Etter pulled them in close and the wonderful biscuit-odor of their hair filled her nose. "How's Lenny?" she asked Peter.

"Good. We decided to get together at your place."

She was not surprised, surprised. They were oddly dependent for children who'd moved thousands of miles away; yet they'd complained and complained that she and Jack should have bought a bigger place in the foothills. She and Jack had liked the guards, the main wall thick with vines, green lawns all around them, their courtyard full of roses and citrus and hibiscus.

"Lenny brought some godawful vegetarian casserole. Looks like kitty litter, or what goes in it," Peter said. The children, four and six, giggled. Etter murmured a slight reproval meant half in fun; they didn't understand, they went silent. She thought she might make up by placing her rather natty hat on Peter's head; but suppose the surprise startled him, and they all ended up crushed by oncoming cars? Her grandchildren crushed, her grown son —child she watched cross streets for years, as if eyes had the power to stop the arrival of disaster — and herself, herself crushed, too.

"Mommy bought hot dogs," her granddaughter said. Said Peter, "And buns. She's making a salad. Lenny's got some friend with her she wants you to meet." He made a little face; the presence of the granchildren stopped Etter from asking why.

* * *

Lenny met Etter with hugs by the service entrance. "Well, look at this skinny!" she said. Except for her guest, who waited at a polite but unshy distance in the kitchen, the others were upstairs watching *The Muppet Show.*

"Hello," Etter called into the guest.

"This is Eleanor, Mother," said Lenny.

"Welcome to the land of the sun!" said Eleanor: skin opulently desert-worn, skirt bearing a turquoise firebird, wonderful heavy bun resting on her shoulders, natural as a knot in a tree. By comparison, Etter, in her navy Ultrasuede, felt diminished, a fuddy-dud.

"Your Lenny's such a joy!" Eleanor said, taking Lenny's hand. Lenny smiled, unabashedly proud of Eleanor's recommendations. Etter smiled back; they certainly meant for her to share in this, but she felt left out. Eleanor was probably not much younger than herself, yet Lenny saw Eleanor as a friend. Maybe she even talked to Eleanor about sex. Sex. With Jack gone, Etter found herself neuter to the world. A little rag of anger dropped through her, top to bottom, making her feet ache.

"Somebody's painted my kitchen!" She stepped closer to the walls, now a peach-adobe color and not the pale cream she'd had them painted on her last visit.

"I did them," said Lenny.

"Very nice," Etter said, trying to squeeze Lenny's feelings in with her own dismay. Peach walls.

"Scotch and water, Mother?" Peter asked. She nodded, but really only to avoid being odd man out; having a drink seemed almost wild to her with Jack gone. She'd never even had a drink before she married Jack, a fact the children laughed over, but of which she was proud.

"Eleanor owns Casa del Sol, Mom," said Lenny. "You remember that wonderful shop on the edge of town, all the *true* Indian baskets and pots?"

Probably she did. Very small. Very expensive. "Did this come from your shop?" she asked, shyly fingering Eleanor's beautiful rose shawl.

"Do you like it?" Eleanor whisked the thing from her shoulders. "Put it on! Here, here. It's wonderful on her, isn't it? That color with your skin!"

Lenny nodded. Peter handed Etter her drink. "You're sure you don't feel like The Berry Lady?" he said.

"The Berry Lady!" Lenny cried. Etter felt her cheeks redden. She shrugged away from the cloth with a little laugh: The Berry Lady was a quaint, shawled woman who had made her way along the lakeshore of the children's childhood.

"Okay, okay, not The Berry Lady," Peter said, and tugged the cloth back onto Etter's shoulders, his shame making her even more uncomfortable; she had to stand still, let him, not make a scene.

* * *

"It won't seem nearly so hot if you tear up the carpet and expose that gorgeous tile," Lenny said over dinner. Etter knew Lenny hoped to make the change sound practical rather than aesthetic; the subject had been broached before, and Jack had been opposed. The children were careful not to say things which might seem like a charge against Jack, not to imply his death had set her free. They had loved their father — better than they loved her, she suspected — but they had no idea what his death meant. Down the long glass table, the candlelit faces of children, grandchildren, and Lenny's handsome guest glowed like the luminarias the inhabitants set along their drives at Christmas. Forks scraped over the rough pottery she and Jack had bought in Nogales. The children, her children didn't understand that the lines slowly

84

gathering on their faces were not going to disappear. With all their talk of diet and exercise, they seemed to think they could turn the clock around, or at least keep it from moving once they got the proper routine down: everything was still possible.

In the bathroom, before dinner, while Etter coated her lips with Vaseline — everything dried out down here! — Lenny had said, "Do you know, Mother, every twelve years your body is composed of entirely different cells than the cells it had twelve years before?" She put her arm around Etter — it was nice, how they were all more affectionate now. She said, as if it should be a great comfort, "Just think, Mom, when you're sixty-nine, you'll be an entirely new person!" Sixty-nine. The children had thoughtfully cleared Jack's things from the closets but they'd missed the medicine chest. Etter closed the door quickly on the bottle of British Sterling, the toenail clippers on a chain.

Etter worried about Lenny. She'd been married and divorced twice. She had a child with each ex-husband, which meant enormously difficult holiday arrangements, flights, the hubbub of two red-faced fathers sometimes arriving for visitation pickups at the same time. She was working at the Desert Museum on a CETA grant, but she had expensive tastes. She had brought with her, that evening, in addition to Eleanor and the boys, a round of Stilton — Etter had never purchased Stilton in her life — but when Etter thanked her, Lenny winked and handed Etter the register tape, clearly expecting reimbursement. "I did bring the tabouli, though," she said.

Now Lenny smiled down the table at Etter, trying to ignore a quarrel between her sons. Recently, she had written Etter an impassioned letter quoting a book whose central thesis was that every woman was a daughter. The letter was fenced with exclamation marks and sadness; Etter thrilled to its intensity, but didn't know how to respond. If she sent her a gift, she would have to send Peter a gift, and that would invalidate the one to Lenny. She tried to give Lenny a special smile; they lifted their wine glasses to one another in the same movement, a private toast.

"Has Eleanor told you she's going to Spain, Mother?" Lenny asked after they had regained a moist sort of composure.

"Next month," Eleanor said. "And I *still* haven't found anyone to work the shop with Tina while I'm gone.¡ *Si que fue un disastre!*"

"Mother has to meet Tina. You'd love Tina, Mom," Lenny said.

"Etter's been to Spain," said Peter's wife.

"How marvelous! Where?" Eleanor dipped further over the table, after a new view of Etter. Etter rummaged for a few names besides Madrid and Barcelona. "Torremolinos. Granada. Malaga." The foreign pronunciations made her shy and she said them in a breathy, uncharacteristic voice.

"I'm going to Granada! Did you get to Toledo?" Eleanor pulled her chair out and dragged it to Etter's side.

"Toledo, yes," said Etter.

With the wine and everyone trying so hard to be a family, Etter could hardly help but connect working at Eleanor's Casa del Sol with possession of Eleanor's bristling good looks and air of competency — and of Lenny's obvious admiration of her. When the subject of the shop came round again, as Etter knew it would — Lenny seemed to have set the thing up this way — Etter was ready to demonstrate that she knew a shaky thing or two about the crafts of the region. Lenny nodded and beamed at "Zuni inlay," "ceremonial jar," "Kachina," and when the offer came, Etter said yes.

"Wonderful!" Eleanor said, and, giddy, Etter carried a platter out to her peach kitchen. Well, she would not be like some widows. There had been a visit to Peter when he was in law school: in the hall of his apartment house, a shrunken woman with wild points of hair wept and screamed. Her children and grandchildren were carrying her things up to the apartment. She shouted, "I won't stay! You can't make me!" Like a child pleading with her parents before they float off into a night on the town.

Lenny stayed after the others left, her boys asleep on the big bed down the hall. She helped Etter wash up the dishes. "I'm glad you're here," she told Etter.

"You can move in with me if you need to," Etter said, but she knew that Lenny knew it wouldn't work.

"I'll think about it," Lenny said. With a damp hand, she gathered Etter's chin-length hair towards the nape of her neck, then stepped in front of Etter to check the effect. "Very handsome!" she murmured. Etter, looking at her reflection in the window over the sink, smiled for Lenny, but was not so sure.

* * *

The shop was on the edge of town. Cars drove by quickly, eager to make a getaway. Sometimes, passing drivers frightened her with their sudden stops, the popping gravel pushed into crescents by their tires. Generally, trips to the shop were planned, but the exterior of the building was so unimposing — a gas station built several decades in anticipation of the automobile? — customers were likely to drive by before realizing their error.

Etter sunk deeper into the thick oatmeal sweater she had given Jack last Christmas. Dense, almost as if woven from paper, it was the only thing which really kept her warm. The winter chill of the shop, the single space heater, low ceilings and small windows, the incandescents and troughs of pots made her think of her mother's basement storeroom, one wall holding empty fruit jars, one holding full, seasonally balanced.

Before her sat a mug of instant coffee and a book on the fetishes of the Southwest (better examples of the items in the display case under her elbows). She pared tiny bits off an apple. An apple would last her till dinner these days. She set the mug on one corner of the book, her elbow on the other, so she could study the fetishes of the six directions while she chipped on the apple. Lately, when she tried to imagine Jack's face, it seemed to slide towards the edge of her brain, where it warped, almost like the photo of "Brown Bear of the West," tucked too close to the spine of the book. Mountain Lion. Eagle. She liked the cool stone figures very much, but thought belief in them dangerous: what would you do if you lost that container of good fortune? As

Eleanor had said, "*¡Si que fue un disastre!*"

Etter still wasn't used to the door bell, and she gasped at its ring. No one had told her the shop would always be kept locked — "against the undesireables," as Tina Bartlett said. Tina Bartlett had worked in the shop for nine years.

A pair of women, husbands waiting outside in a Buick, filed past Etter when she opened the door. Fat car, Etter thought, and was surprised at herself. "Fat car" sounded like something one of her children might have said back in the Sixties. *She* owned a Buick, an Electra 225 which Jack had given her. I'm mad at him! she thought. Mad at Jack!

"Can we help you?" Tina Bartlett called from the backroom, her cue irritating Etter. The women demurred. They looked at Etter as if they did not know how to place her. Tina Bartlett stuck her head out the curtain to the backroom, said, "Okey-doke!" and made the women smile.

Tina Bartlett was small with steel gray hair curled tight as a poodle's. Jack would have called Tina a character. He would have smiled as he said it, but Etter would have known he dismissed Tina, relegated her to a lumber room of other useless people. Tina was divorced. She once said to Etter, "Some people call theirs an Ex, but I call mine a Why." Then she spanked her skinny knees and laughed and laughed. Before Etter's time, she once chased a gunman out of the store. She liked to tell customers about the incident, making the scene sound fraught, simultaneously, with danger and comedy:

"I was taking my lunch out of the thermos bag under the counter. I looked up when this fellow came in. Something was wrong with his face, but I'm being polite, I look away. Turned out he had a nylon stocking over his head!" Everyone laughed at this point of the story; Tina gave them a chance before continuing. "'You've got to be kidding!' I said. 'You just back on out the door.'" At that point, Tina pulled a gun out from the box of ribbons under the display case of fetishes and jewelry, set the customers gasping. "I showed him this," she said, "and you better believe he took off running." She grinned. "*That's* why we lock up."

Whenever the children called Etter now, they asked about Tina, as if she and Etter were great friends, did outrageous things together; but Tina Bartlett already had a best friend. Her initials were DDT, and when the two called each other, there was giggling. "DDT here! Is TB here?" Etter thought them silly beyond belief, though she would not have minded a monicker. Her initials were hopeless: EJM. And what could be done with *Etter*?

And what on earth good was a shop with a locked door? One of the fun things about a shop was an air of hospitality. The locked door made her feel endangered. How was she to know who to open it to? "Don't go to the door, then, Mother," Lenny had told her. "Just go in the back."

"I can't very well go in the back if somebody's at the door."

"Just shake your head, like you're closed."

On Etter's first day of work, a large van had pulled up in front of the shop, music pouring from its innards, and out climbed three men, black, dressed in the closest thing to zoot suits Etter could remember ever seeing in the light of day. Two of them — a big man, handsome, and a skinny one in lime green — were already at the door by the time she stood up. They left the van running; the third fellow, in sober brown, with an International Harvester hat on his head, stayed beside the van, smoking.

"Good day," the handsome man had said. He sported a large ring which winked at Etter when he picked up a pot. She moved behind the counter, her hand hovering over the ribbon box. The men spent twenty-one hundred dollars in fifteen minutes. That evening, she saw a photo of the trio in the entertainment section of the paper. Jazz musicians. Tickets for twelve-fifty. She had never told anyone *that* story.

The women from the Buick — West Virginia plates — edged their way through the shop, pretended to be discreet in their exclamations over the price tags, but were not. Tina emerged from the backroom, a jaunty cap on her head: creamy llama wool with bittersweet llamas circling the brim. "I'm running to the P.O. Have fun," she said as she went out the door.

Etter sliced deeper into the apple, exposing its creamy halo. She would not wear Jack's sweater again. "Save it," that's what he would have said, but he wasn't here.

One of the women, chocolate scarf knotted high on her throat, brought a pot to the counter. "Is this right?" she asked, glancing back at her friend with raised eyebrows.

"Six hundred and fifty. Yes. That's a ceremonial jar." Etter repeated, almost verbatim, the decidedly inaccurate speech Tina Bartlett had offered on another pot that very morning. She was greatly relieved when the woman carried the pot back to its place and turned to something else.

What if Lenny had somehow overheard?

There was too much to learn, it swam by her, quick and dark as schools of baby bullheads moving under her dock on White Bear. The only book she seemed to have absorbed was one Tina Bartlett gave her: *Black Elk Speaks.* Etter couldn't make heads nor tails of Black Elk's great vision, but she understood his sorrow over it not coming to fruition. "It is time! It is time!" the skies cried to Black Elk, but he did not know what he was meant to do. Poor Black Elk. And though he spoke about a scalping the way Etter might a sighting of a Great Horned Owl, he saved the lives of children, he wept, he used the Oglala name for the months: Moon When The Plums Turn Purple; Moon Of The Black Cherries. Etter had lived that way, too, once upon a time. Life began over every September with the buying of school shoes and woolens; and then there was planning for Halloween costumes, Thanksgiving dinner, and so on. Black Elk's story ended after the Battle of Wounded Knee, but he lived many, many years beyond that time.

Etter massaged her temples as the other woman, this one with a sprig of holly attached to her lapel, approached the counter. The holly was real; several of its points were already broken off. Christmas was coming. Etter kept forgetting. At home, the goldfinches at her feeder would be in their drab. She'd have regular visits from cardinals, passing cluster of the almost exotic cedar waxwings. Here, the pale adobe houses looked odd in festive lights, more like honky-tonks or juke boxes than homes. The children wanted her to try an Arizona-style Christmas this year: mass at The San Xavier Mission, a turkey roast in Sabino Canyon. Last week, with all of them gathered for dinner, she'd said, "I'd fly us all home?" She smiled so nobody would become angry if they thought the idea dumb.

"This is home," Peter had said. Lenny nodded. She had a new boyfriend with her. She wore harem pants tucked into Majorette boots with dirty tassels. The boyfriend was with the FBI. "Oh," Etter said at the news, and decided then and there she would have to talk to Lenny. Things weren't so desperate, she'd tell the girl, thirty-one wasn't so old. Before dinner, the FBI man showed Etter his gun and holster, and, with some ceremony, requested permission to set it on top of the buffet. Throughout the meal, Etter found herself eyeing the nub of leather, extended over the top shelf like the nose of some shy but curious animal.

"How much is that?" The woman with the holly pointed to a travertine sheep with a chip of turquoise tied to its back. At least Etter *thought* it was a sheep. She wasn't complaining, but didn't even the bears look swinish in a pleasant sort of way? She placed the fetish into the woman's hand. One delight was holding the smooth, cool figures. They felt like the Japanese pebbles she used in flower arrangements. Peter used to secret those rocks on his tongue, they soothed him.

"The power is supposedly in the spirit that lives in the fetish, and not in the fetish itself," Etter said. Feeling suddenly friendly, she held out a jet bear with turquoise Orphan Annie eyes, a coral heart-line running along its side. "This is my favorite." In back, she was working on a model desert to insert in the case; she had built that bear its own cave.

Clutching their hairdos, the women ran back to the Buick. Etter touched the ends of her own hair, which now almost reached her shoulders. The women shook their heads at the husbands: an opinion of the prices, Etter supposed. They could easily have been herself and Marilyn Eggert with Jack and Lee Eggert waiting in the car.

She went into the backroom, a cubbyhole with a hot plate, a table full of packaging materials. Tina Bartlett had stapled a postcard from Eleanor onto the curtain. The handwriting was so large the card said little more than hello.

The rose-patterned sheet Etter used as a cover for the model stuck on the highest points of the salt clay, and she had to tug at the cloth to remove it.

She pulled a bag from her purse: poster paints, a brush. The shop's quiet was a mixed blessing: she did not have to go to the door, she did have to be alone. She held down the panic by working. She painted. She made lakes — one sheet of aluminum foil, one sheet of green tissue paper, one sheet of blue; she'd learned the trick helping the children through social studies years before.

By the time she pulled away from the shop, it was already five-thirty. Peter had helped her devise a route to the house which would keep her off busy roads; tonight it seemed too slow. She felt hungry, truly hungry for the first time in months. She was so hungry the feeling almost scared her. Mentally, she ticked through the contents of the freezer, decided on an Oriental-style TV dinner.

Her headlights washed over winter-bleached zoysia, rocks, palm trees, houses pale and clean as igloos. "Stop For Golf Carts!" said a sign. There were fewer green lawns than when she and Jack had bought in. "People are finally getting smart about the water table and switching to desert plantings," Peter explained. "You ought to do the same."

From behind the gate house, the guard's cart pressed into the road, aligned itself with Etter's window. Etter set her face in a mildly puzzled look; cool, unimpeachable, patient. Her window whined its way into the door, stopped with a small *thuck*. She smiled at the guard.

"How're you this evening, ma'am?"

"Just fine, thank you."

"Can I help you with something here?" He shined his flashlight into the backseat, then onto the passenger seat, looking.

"I live here," Etter said. With only the pressure of her left index finger, she erected a glass wall between herself and the guard. She drove further in. The slow yawn of the electric garage door welcomed her home.

* * *

"Talk about The Painted Desert!" said Tina Bartlett. Etter slid the sections of her model into the display case without a word. Some of the paint came off on her palms, leaving them green. Maybe she *had* overdone things a bit. The light in the backroom had not been good.

Tina slipped on her jacket, preparing for her trip to the post office. "I'm going to have to take you for a little nature hike, dear," she said, shaking her head at the model.

"You've made your point," said Etter, and was surprised at her tone. She certainly didn't want to spoil things with Tina, or give Tina fodder for poor-sport remarks. She set a bear in a depression — almost a cave — situated on one of the model's higher peaks. The bear alone made the model look like one of those amphitheaters of fake rock which zoos use to house big animals; she added a pair of eagles, a sheep of ground beans and flour, a travertine coyote and wolf, another bear, and two turquoise moles. She made sure to say a cheery good-bye to Tina, as if not a thing in the world were wrong between them. Maybe she should invite Tina to supper. No. She'd invited Lenny over for that talk. "Lenny," she would say, very gentle, "it is no crime for you and the boys to live alone."

Around noon, a station wagon bearing Iowa plates pulled up, and a complete family hatched from its doors.

"Hello!" Etter called out to them; even before they had a chance to ring, she was letting them in. She glanced outside as the family — four children from perhaps seven to fifteen — filed past her. Half proud, half shy, she said to the parents, "Iowa!", as if just making the discovery. "Why, we're practically neighbors. I'm from Minnesota!"

They were nice people. And not only were they sailors, they'd been housed at Garsts' in White Bear during the last regatta! A small world, they said, and smiled and shook their heads over the fact. She showed the littlest girl the cheap items — small eyes of the gods, Mexican tops and chocolate mixers, Christmas ornaments fashioned from bread dough and tin can lids. She might suggest the shop get more things like that, fill big good-looking baskets with things picked up in Nogales. That brown sugar confection in tiny pans. Sour balls. The picture made her almost laugh aloud: herself running a kind of old-time candy counter!

"Maybe we'll meet again!" she said gaily. She could invite them to dinner, to meet the children. She could tell them Tina Bartlett's story as if it were her own.

"Look," the smallest child said, peering at the model while her dad paid for a handful of Christmas ornaments: a star, a sun, an angel. "*Look.*"

The father nodded absently; "Like Minnesota," he said. He winked at Etter. "Land of Ten Thousand Lakes."

Already the rest of the family was climbing into the car.

"Tell the lady thank you."

He held the door open for the child. Before it swung closed, a stringy-haired girl of perhaps sixteen caught it — Etter thought for a second of Lenny back in her days of grime-hemmed blue jeans — and then the girl was in, followed by a boy. Too late. Beneath their shoes, the inevitable scatter of fine sand scoured the floorboards. The boy curved himself over one of the high troughs of pots. His hair was pale blond with pink scalp showing through. He flipped up a price tag. "Hh!" he said.

Etter looked down at the book on the counter — a buzzing spread of Zuni bird necklaces — and her knees jiggled against the undersides of the glass case. What was the girl eating? One of those juicy desert fruits: cheri-moya. "What're them things?" the girl asked, pointing to the fetishes, dripping a little juice on the case. Dear, Etter thought she might say. Dear.

"How come you got a doorbell?" the girl asked. "We seen a doorbell."

Etter began to answer, but then she could not remember the question. It was something about the boy. The boy was turned away from the counter. He was reaching into his jacket for something. As if she had lived with it all her life, Etter recognized the fumbling, the red threat of his neck.

By the time he turned to the counter, she had the gun, pink ribbon dangling from its barrel, aimed. The boy dropped what was in his hand — a cigarette lighter — and it skipped across the floor. The cigarette he had been preparing to light clung to his lower lip as if glued there.

"Oh," Etter said, sorry, sorry, sorry and bewildered, "you can't smoke in here."

"Just hang on there, lady," the boy said, and gave the girl a little shove. "We're going."

She stood behind the counter for a moment, her lungs cold, subaqueous, light as the pale balloons of tissue the children used to drag home after somebody killed a carp.

"Wait!"

Outside, the wind whipped her hair across her mouth. She called into the brush, through ocotillos and thin air, "I thought you had a gun, I'm sorry." A roadrunner, typically lunatic, scrambled across a clear spot and froze. Then nothing. The crackling of rocks and dry vegetation beneath her feet so loud, so intimately crisp she might have been chewing up the stuff rather than walking on it. She pushed back a feathery green branch and it gave off an oily smell, pungent as the stack of fence posts on her parents' farm. "I'm sorry," she called again; but she did not want to frighten them any more than she already had. She headed back to the shop, gun heavy in her hand.

She tried the door but, of course, she was locked out. "Oh, hell," she said, "hell." And looked about as if help might be at her elbow, waiting to hand her the key. But there was nothing, only that desert light — so clear it might have been sifted — desert light holding the desert.

She peered through a window at the dark cozy shop. In the glass case, the animals kept a stiff and constant watch from the hills and valleys of their land. Eagles. Sheep. Coyotes. Bears. The troughs, the pots and baskets, a packing crate losing its excelsior — everything inside glowed like something secret or accidentally lost. Through the shop and out another window, she could see the Santa Catalinas, peaks cropped by the window frame. The mountains seemed to go and on, to fill her vision like some monster so fierce, so enormous it did not need to flex muscles or bare teeth.

She let her eyes close for a moment. Her heartbeat was beginning to slow. She imagined herself driving alone up the long precipitous road which led to the mountains' highest peak, up that road which Jack and the children had once driven her, first past cactus and yucca, then pines, arriving, finally, at snow. But for now she would have to wait for Tina Bartlett to come back. She would have to hide the gun. Or invent her own story. She supposed she could do that.

SMALL ACTS

Carl throws the wok lid across the kitchen and into the dining room. It hits the carpet with a dull gong. Appropriate, Melanie thinks, sort of oriental-sounding. Carl's dog, an immense German shepherd, bounds up the stairs from the basement, circles the lid warily, and sniffs at it as if it were a turtle or any mysterious animal.

"Just a minute," Melanie says into the phone. She covers the mouthpiece with her free hand. "I'll be off in two seconds," she tells Carl. She feels so happy in his jealousy that she smiles, and, believing all happiness to be something lovers should share, is almost surprised when Carl doesn't smile in return.

"Get off, now," he says. His voice is dull. She tries to see his face, to check out the threat, but he's busy over the bent pan lid.

The man on the phone is telling Melanie about a trip he's making to Colombia, but she isn't listening. "Ooo ..." she says to his itinerary, figures, enthusiasm. "Hmm," when he tells her about the problems he's had with traveler's checks in Jamaica. The dog pads into the kitchen and noses her from behind. She swats at the air over its head in annoyance. "Shoo, shoo," she says.

Carl presses on opposite sides of the domed lid, his face red with the effort. Show of strength, Melanie thinks. An ugly Y of vein rises on his forehead, making her feel both tender and frightened towards him.

She thinks he's beautiful — that he looks like the perfectly designed table knife. A table knife, Scandinavian, or, maybe, a bone from a whale, some important piece of a monster-sized whole. She puts her hand over the mouthpieces again and steps into the dining room. "Hey, Crusher," she says softly. She thinks he might laugh, might stop pushing on the metal and let the veins return to normal.

He claps the lid down on the table and she runs back into the kitchen. The lid begins to spin, but its own dull weight stops it. She feels almost sorry for the table — that monstrous cup of air fixed to it and nothing to be done, like having a huge seashell bonded to your ear forever. Carl told her once that the noise she heard in seashells was the sound of blood rushing through the brain. She wondered if he told her that to frighten her; but, no, she decided it was just like him to imagine physical turmoil inside her head. She told him there was a better reason, something about air spiralling from seashell to ear and back again.

"Get off the phone," Carl says.

She crooks the receiver deeper into her shoulder, covers it with both hands. She drags it and the long, black cord across the kitchen. "Listen, I'm going to have to hang up in a second."

Carl comes to the kitchen doorway, "Now!" he says. She smiles, nods, yes, yes, she's getting off, just one minute. He reaches into the kitchen and presses down the metal cradle.

"Hey!" she says. Carl holds his hand out for the receiver, like a tough cop asking for a lunatic's weapon. "I can't believe you did that, man." She considers whacking his restraining hand with the phone, but decides this wouldn't be wise.

"Don't call me 'man,' " he says.

"Oh, man." She rolls her eyes ceilingward. As if she is some casual litterer out for a stroll, she spreads her fingers and releases the receiver. It hits the floor with a crack which she doesn't allow her face to register, but she worries: Did she hurt it? Will it work now?

That these small acts of violence can be done always amazes Melanie. In college, at a party, she leaned over and bit into a boyfriend's thigh when she thought he flirted with another woman. Later than night, she clapped her hands in shame and delight over his bruise — a somber rainbow of yellow, green, and purple. Once, during a fight with Carl, she picked up a full plate of coleslaw, fish and rice, lifted it high and sent it smashing to the floor. She watched the cabbage, the rice, and chunks of pottery rise up and settle, watched Carl move from the table, put on his coat, say, "That does it." It was all a surprise to her, but she did recover; she grabbed him tight about the neck — to get away he would have had to drag her down the street with him, and, then, she thought, all he really would have escaped was the house, the mess on the floor.

Because she cannot think of anything else to say, she repeats, "I can't believe you did that, man." The phone begins signalling its abandonment. The noise makes her think of disasters: of something coming up behind you fast, film clips of World War I air raids, the white smears of faces running through streets of drizzle and fear. She hates the sound, but she smiles. She's not about to pick up the phone. Let it cry all night long.

Down the hall and into the bedroom she goes. He follows. She flops onto the mattress, pats it with her hand. "Come here," she says. He stands at the end of the bed, frowning. He wears swim trunks, and, with his arms folded tight across his chest, looks like a gangly wrestler. "Come here," she says again.

"No thanks."

She raises her eyebrows, lifts herself up on her elbows. Her pajamas are green silk, piped in white and tailored like a man's; she thinks they give her a wholesome look, seductive in its own right. She crawls to the foot of the bed and tugs at the hem of his swim trunks. "Carl, I didn't *do* anything."

"I thought we were through with that little game, Melanie." He steps back from the bed, but she holds onto the trunks. "Would you get your hands off me, please," he says, and she lets go. "So who was it?"

She knows that the best thing to do would be to answer immediately, casually, but she can't say the name, she's not sure enough of what Carl's reaction will be.

"Who was it, damn it?"

"Chris," she says quickly. "It was just Chris."

"I told you I didn't want any of those guys calling anymore. I thought we had this all straightened out."

"I didn't ask him to call," she says.

"So why did you talk to him?"

Why did she talk to him? It would be nice if she could tell Carl that the calls are for him, that they're little gifts, and that she knows he wants her to get them forever and ever, and forever and ever to be there while she tells the callers, "But I'm not interested in you." She knows this. Before he moved in, he always smiled and shook his head when he handed her the phone and the caller was a man. Impressed, impressed, yes, he was. He thought she was wild and crazy and wonderful — living all alone with a case of beer in the refrigerator, a trust fund, men calling and dropping by. He took her to noisy parties and abandoned her to the first man who asked her to dance. She would look for him and there he'd be, at the outer edge, watching. He might smile at her or lift his glass; she'd smile back, feeling frantic while some stranger twirled her over the lawn and asked where she lived. Then the music might slow; Carl would come up out of the dark and sweep her away with a passion so public it made her face burn with embarrassment and joy. He was tender and charming. Princess, angel, beauty, he whispered in her ear. "It's wonderful to watch you," he said at such a party, and, for the first time, "I love you."

Now he acts stern. He taps a bare foot on the bedroom floor impatiently.

"Humpf. Humpf," Melanie says, imitating Shirley Temple imitating a gruff old man. "Look, I was just saying hello. He's a nice little guy and I was just saying hello." Little, little, this sounds familiar. Teeny-tiny. Not even a real man at all, just teeny-weeny. His weinie's teeny. She smiles, almost begins to laugh. She can't help herself.

Carl kicks the end of the bed. "Stop smiling! Jesus, you're so naive. These guys don't call you for no reason."

"Come here," she says, certain that if he'd just lie down, everything would be fine.

"No!" He leans up against the wall, eyes narrowed, lower lip thrust forward. Like a juvenile delinquent, she thinks, and almost begins laughing again.

She rolls over onto her stomach; if she can't stop the terrible smiles, at least she can hide them from Carl. "I don't see why you have to sound so accusatory," she says.

"There's no such word as 'accusatory.' It makes you sound stupid when you make up words."

She knows just how his lip is curled in disdain. Accusatory. Accusatory. Of course there's such a word as accusatory, isn't there?

Choke chain rattling, the dog enters the room. It butts Melanie in the head and she laughs, flattered by the attention. Usually, she avoids the dog; it's nice enough, but it's too big, it knocks her down when she steps into the backyard, it drags her when she puts it on a leash.

She takes the dog's heavy head in her hands and rubs her nose against its nose. "Cleopatra eyes," she says. "Pretty dog."

"Get out, Tristan!" Carl yells at the dog. "Out!" He shoves the dog from the room with both hands, kicks at the air behind it.

"Carl," she says, quietly, disapproving.

"You shut up. You encourage that creep to call you," he says. "Do you have to get attention from every little jerk that comes along?"

This is what he doesn't understand, she thinks: it takes work. No matter how attractive you are, it takes work, and now that she won't sleep with them anymore, the work is harder, almost exhausting.

She lifts herself onto her elbows and addresses the headboard. "Are you insulting me, Carl?" There's a warble in her voice which she recognizes as the first step towards tears, but she takes it back, trades it in on something else.

"Yes, I'm insulting you, of course I am. I'd think you'd be embarrassed, the way you act. 'I spread my legs for the sun.' Jesus. And everybody at the whole fucking pool turns to listen. 'I spread my legs for the sun.'"

"In case you don't remember, dear, all those people turned because they wanted to hear my answer to your loving question, 'How the fuck did the insides of your thighs get so tan?' I gave you exactly the answer you were asking for."

She thinks she's explained this so well, tit for tat, that there isn't even a need to be angry anymore. "'I spread my legs for the sun,'" she says, laughing and shaking her head. She rolls onto her back. Carl looks sad, mad, sad and mad, but it's his own fault. She closes her eyes and concentrates very hard on making him come lie down. Lie down. Lie down and kiss me.

"Sometimes I think you *like* to cause trouble between us, Melanie," he says.

"Not me."

He slides down the wall until he's seated on his haunches. He stares out over her, like a farmer contemplating his bad fields. It saddens Melanie to see how he works his jaw back and forth, grinding his teeth. "You like to make up, maybe. I don't know what it is," he says.

"Some people think I'm rather nice," she says, and holds her arms out to him.

"I guess you're lucky about that," he says, "because you make *me* sick."

The words are so automatic that she winces. She grabs great clumps of her curly hair. "Well, my goodness, dear, you must know I'm totally mad!" She gnashes her teeth. The bed rattles in its frame as she pummels the mattress with heels and fists. "Mad, mad, mad!"

Pure gesture, she tells herself when he slams the bedroom door. The only time the door is ever closed is when he's away and she's sleeping by herself. He did it to make me lonely, she thinks, and resents his success. She sees herself a mouth, the whole of her a mouth, moving like a half-track through some cartoon landscape, her needs hideous.

The back door opens, closes. She runs to the living room. "Hey, hey,

Tristan," she hears Carl's voice, soft and sweet. Outside, the dog stands with its muddy forepaws on Carl's shoulders, dancing the man backwards. In spite of Melanie's protests, Carl bought the animal a wading pool. "To keep him cool," Carl said. Melanie looks at the muddy circle surrounding the pool, the tracks worn in the lawn. "Pig wallow," she says aloud. "A fucking pig wallow." The dog's belly and lower legs are always wet, its fur hanging in slick pointed clumps. Like seaweed, she thinks, and it stinks.

Sometimes, when Carl is out of town on business, and she opens the gate to bring Tristan in for the night, the dog runs off. She will call after it half-heartedly, half-glad to see it go; but then she remembers, she's afraid to sleep alone in the house; she remembers that Carl will blame her, like the time that the dog pushed through the front screen and sunk its teeth into the mailman's arm. So she puts her coat over her pajamas and drives around the neighborhood, the car door open. Eventually, the dog will come, panting up out of the night, and she'll brace herself for the moment when all that weight and wet fur bounds across her lap and into the car.

* * *

"Down," Carl says, and, laughing, pushes the dog away.

No doubt, Melanie thinks, he's illustrating how much fun, what a good guy he is, just in case I'm watching. No doubt. And he doesn't do it just for me, no, even if I weren't here, he'd do it, he'd show *himself* what a fun-loving guy he is.

The dog runs a circle around the yard, splashes through the pool, lifts its leg to one of Melanie's tomato plants.

"Don't do that, you jerk!" she screams out the window.

"Here, Tristan," Carl calls. He kneels, rubs the animal's ears. "You're a good dog, aren't you? Good dog," he croons.

"Look at nice Carl," Melanie says. She knows he can't hear her, but still takes pleasure in speaking the words aloud. "What a good boy he is. Nice Carl. Good boy, Carl." She sticks her tongue out at him. He rises, walks out of her view. "Carl, Carl, where are you going?" she whispers. She flattens her nose to the kitchen screen, but she can't see him. The whine of water and pump going on sends a shiver through the house, and Carl reappears, walking a long, green hose across the lawn. He fills the dog's bowl, the murky pool. The kitchen ceiling picks up the reflection, rocks with the shimmer of water and light. Just like we live near the ocean, Melanie thinks, in a wonderful house perched over the ocean or even on a lake. The water's shine always leaves her feeling cheated, as if it were a promise given, then retracted.

She walks to the back of the house, latches the screen door, then locks the inner door. She congratulates herself on thinking of the screen. Carl always says anyone could stick a fist right through the glass of the inner door, reach in and enter. He says, regularly, he's going to change that door, put up something solid. She says nothing, but when he's gone, she's afraid. Her nightgown brushing against her thigh as she crawls into bed makes her turn in terror. She waits for the sound of breaking glass, footsteps — would they come fast or slow, pounding through the house and throwing the door open, or would there be nothing, then a hand over the mouth?

* * *

She locks the front door; a slab of hardwood, she thinks happily. In her elbows and knees she feels small vacancies, little hollows of fear that make her keep a hand on the walls as she moves towards the bedroom. The room is dark, the bamboo curtains down. The light coming through the curtains makes the room, with its collection of plants — *de rigueur*, she thinks — seem almost tropical. There was a movie once, she remembers, a couple was in Africa, in a room much like this. The man and woman had argued. The man pushed the woman down the stairs. There was a miscarriage, Melanie thinks, or maybe not, maybe she was overlaying *Gone With the Wind*. And did he push her or did she fall? Melanie can only remember the frightening tumble of the woman's pale safari clothes, the still body at the base of the stairs.

At the sound of the back gate swinging to, her blood rushes. Nothing. She goes down the hall, checks the living-room. Not there, not in the kitchen, not in the backyard.

"Keys, keys," she thinks, suddenly frightened, but they hang on their peg over the sink.

* * *

Carl sits on the front steps reading the evening paper. She presses her hot forehead to the living room window. "Dear Abby" he's reading. "Dear Abby" and the funnies. She finds it so endearing that he reads "Dear Abby" that she almost unlocks the door. He wouldn't even have to know. But maybe he's already tried the door and he's just waiting for her to unlock it. Maybe he's not going to acknowledge it. Still, if he doesn't know now, what's he going to do when he does?

He shakes the paper out and begins reading the sports page. She almost raps on the glass. She can't see his face, but, of course, she thinks sadly, even if he did turn around, she wouldn't necessarily understand what he's thinking.

He stands, folds the paper, and though she wants to open the door, he's already starting up the steps and there isn't time, it isn't safe. She runs to the bathroom and locks it, crouching down, rocking on her heels and laughing. "Oh, Carl, Carl," she says, and she shivers.

There is the rattle of the front door, then quiet; the sound of the back door being tried, then banged. How horribly metal doors thunder inside their metal frames, as if they were made for relaying emotions, but, oh, there's her face in the mirror, and her tan is very becoming, even darker in the fluorescent light!

She lifts her pajama tops, admiring the creamy edge of her breasts where tanned meet untanned, and gives the mirror a smile of seduction. She hopes

Carl won't kick in the screen. He's a quiet man, but he's also unpredictable. The medicine cabinet in the bathroom is a replacement. He tore the mirrored door off the first one. She never said anything about it — it had made her so sad, thinking of him in the bathroom, trying to smash the metal-backed mirror and ending up, in desperation, tearing off the whole door. She knew what a rotten, shameful thing it was to have your dramatic gestures fall flat.

Outside, the dog barks in confusion, the sound moving back and forth across the yard. It splashes through the water, rattles the fence. "Quiet, quiet," Carl says softly, alarming Melanie by his nearness.

It may be dangerous to be in here, she thinks. Such a small space and she might be trapped. She unlocks the door and moves into the kitchen. She takes up a sponge, wets it, wipes a section of counter. Carl is trying the bathroom window; even in the kitchen she can hear his breathing. She imagines him hanging by one hand, no ladder — and it isn't comical, no, it isn't.

She lifts up the toaster and blender and does a thorough job of cleaning, even pouring a little ammonia on a stain before scrubbing with a steel wool pad.

"Get *down*, Tristan." Carl at the window. Tristan. She thinks it's an awful name. Although she hates to think of Carl with anyone else, she's always hoped that the name was something the woman he lived with before dreamed up, that it wasn't entirely his fault.

I wouldn't mind if he went away forever, she thinks. She rests her cheek on the cool, clean counter-top, almost dizzy with the thought. Maybe she could just throw his keys out to him. Maybe he'd just drive away. Of course, he'd have to come back sometime for his things, but she could go out for lunch, make a huge pile for him on the front steps.

And it would be so wonderful! She'd pour herself a glass of wine before dinner, read late in bed. She'd have small parties, only talk on the phone to people she really wanted to talk to. Sometimes, she might meet friends for a drink or dinner, but, as a rule, she would stay at home and make herself simple but nice meals. Salad. An omelette. At the grocery — smiling apologetically to the check-out people — she'd buy single sticks of butter, those half-cartons of eggs.

There would be nothing she'd keep of him. Nothing. When he was all gone, she'd hire professionals in and have the house cleaned completely. "Lysol the walls," she'd tell them. "Do the corners with cotton swabs." Sweet-smelling bundles of sod would be unfurled over the scarred lawn. She'd send her clothes to the cleaners and stay in a motel until everything was like new, *was* new. A Kerry blue terrier, the dog Melanie has wanted all her life, would rest its paws on her knees when she came in the door, skitter across the kitchen; it would curl up at the foot of the bed, and Melanie would sleep all the night through.

The ripping at the back door startles her — Carl, beyond the glass, striking at the screen with a garden trowel. God, God, she doesn't want that face to come in. She runs for his keys. "Here," she says, opening the inner door and pushing them out the ragged tear. She stands back, waiting to watch him go, but his arm comes through the gray of the screen — pale, as if it is penetrating another world. He pushes up the hook with one deft motion, like he's done it from the outside a million times, and he's in, he's in.

He stands before her, shuffling his feet like a boxer, body shining, his breath coming jagged from a slack mouth. She does the only thing she can do, runs at him so hard that they both fall, her on top with the dog sniffing at her hair, kneading her shoulder with its cold nose.

She presses her face to Carl's chest, laughs softly, until the beats of his heart calm and she thinks the fear in her eyes will be unrecognizable; then she lifts herself up on her elbows and kisses his chin. She has always believed that, sometimes, the safest place to be is as close to danger as possible. Put distance between yourself and a threat, and you have to worry over the varieties of camouflage, the time required to fulfill the arc between leap and arrival, the force a blow can gather as it travels towards you.

She scoots herself up his body so that her face hangs over his. His pupils expand slightly as she brings her eyes closer, closer, trying to avoid everything but those small black holes. She's impressed by their elegant constriction and expansion, but, she knows there's nothing to the eyes, they don't tell you anything; they're like cameras inside the brain, and even what seems to be their expression is just the movement of the skin surrounding them.

"Oh, Carl," she says, very low. "It's so dark in there," and hides her head in the crook of his neck.

RELICS

Richard Lansing sits on the front steps of the house he has lived in for the past seventeen months, minus the last five days. He cannot enter the house because he left his key on the motel room dresser. He did this on purpose; by leaving his key behind he can, without lying, tell Katie's mother he had to wait outside until she arrived. He feels he should be spared explaining to her how unbearable it would be for him to walk through the house alone. Also, he wants Mrs. Freer to see he hasn't been inside since the funeral; from what Katie told him of her parents, he's certain they worry over his being in the house unsupervised and imagine him running off with everything of value.

The long walk from the motel has left Richard lightheaded. For a moment, he thinks he's going to be ill, but the feeling backs away. The pearl-gray Cadillac belonging to Katie's mother turns down the quiet street and begins its smooth dreamlike approach.

Richard's rusty Chevrolet sits idle in the parking lot of an uptown garage. The trip to and from the funeral proved too much for it. He rode the last fifteen minutes in a tow truck, now and then looking out the back window and through the crane; his car followed him into the city like a prize fish.

"Two hundred and fifty bucks, bottom line," the mechanic told him. "More likely, three hundred."

"Three hundred?" Richard said. In savings he had seventy-eight dollars, in checking, nineteen. Katie had insisted that he not take a summer job but, instead, loll around before the world got him for good. "This summer, we live on love," she said; "my father will send it." In the end, he agreed, because it was true, it was his last free summer, and they promised each other they'd never take the money again once one of them started teaching.

* * *

Katie's car is somewhere in Dayton. It rolled three times before it stopped and she was dead. On his trip back from the funeral, Richard fixed his mind on how he would *not* look for the spot where it happened; but then it was there, big brown gashes in the green, as though the land were being broken for planting, and Richard thought, it should have looked worse, it should have looked as if it were mined.

* * *

He walks towards Mrs. Freer's car, stopping to pocket a section of Lincoln log that sticks up out of the unmown grass. The toy belongs to Mark,

Katie's three-year-old son. It is light, it bounces against Richard's leg almost imperceptibly. He opens the door for Mrs. Freer. She is a heavy, permanently disheveled woman, sadly mismatched to her elegant car. Richard met her only once before the funeral. The three of them, Katie, Mark, and Richard visited the Freers for a Thanksgiving during which conversations leaned heavily upon the adults' mutual pleasure in the child, and Katie screamed at her mother for asking Richard if there were wedding bells in the future. Richard wishes that he could like the Freers; they are the last link to Katie now that her ex-husband has taken Mark.

"Hello, Richard." Mrs. Freer gives him a hug. The loneliness of being embraced by this stranger is enough to break his heart, and he backs away, holding up a hand; he begins blindly removing cardboard packing boxes from the car.

Richard suspects Mrs. Freer of acting brave, a little tremble at the corners of her smile. Once, when he and Katie were discussing feminine wiles, Katie smiled the same way. "There, you see, *that's* how it's done," she said, and broke the spell by sticking out her tongue.

"But Katie," Richard said, "you've looked that way when we've been fighting."

"Sure," she said. "And sometimes it's real and sometimes it's not and sometimes I don't know which is which."

* * *

"Hot, hot, hot," says Mrs. Freer. Bottom lip stuck out, she blows air from her mouth, making her bangs rise on the draft. She takes Katie's key ring from her puse. "Which one is it?" she asks.

The key to Katie's car is still on the ring; all of these things, Richard tells himself — the house, the keys, almost all of what was there before — remain in spite of her being dead. "It's the brass one," he says, and looks off across the street while Mrs. Freer fumbles with the lock.

The house is filled with a sickening smell of decay and, for a moment, Richard feels frightened and confused; corpse, he thinks, but the idea passes with a shudder. Mrs. Freer sniffs. "Something must be rotting," he says quickly, wanting her to know that he, too, is aware of the stench, that it isn't something that he and Katie and Mark lived with. On the kitchen counter, there is an open carton of cottage cheese. In the compost bucket, fly maggots shift as if magnetized. He dumps the cheese into the bucket and carries it to the heap in the backyard. When he reenters the house, Mrs. Freer is opening windows, moving about with the efficiency of a disapproving nurse sent over by the county.

* * *

After the funeral, the Freers told Richard he didn't need to move right away, that he could stay until the end of the month, but he said no. He and

Katie never liked the house anyway. It was a present from the Freers to Katie and her ex-husband, Paul, and it always made Richard miserable to think of her there (making love, eating meals, tucking Mark into bed) with someone else. Katie found the house an embarrassment; everyone she and Richard knew lived in cramped but interesting old apartments. She said to Richard, "We'll get a place right for us in the fall and it'll have an upstairs and wood and we'll love it." What she wanted was a garden and a porch with a place for a swing — all touchingly banal, he thought. "And a budget," she said, "we'll have a budget." She made a budget sound like a trip to Spain, something exotic they could look forward to sharing.

"Now be sure and take everything you need," Mrs. Freer says. Richard mumbles and sticks his head into the linen closet. He is careful to take only those things he brought when he moved in. One pair of sheets, a few faded towels — it is easy for him to recover his dingy goods from Katie's piles of bright decorator linens. Mrs. Freer reaches into the closet. She is close enough that he can feel her breath on his arm. Her perfume is dense, expensive; it reminds him of someone, but he can get no further than the perfume, a furry coat in a heated car. Mrs. Freer runs her finger up the side of a stack of wash-cloths. "I gave her those, didn't I?" she says and points to a set of cream-colored sheets piped in brown. Richard doesn't answer, doesn't believe that she expects an answer.

* * *

Into the living room he carries a noisy box filled with those kitchen things which are unquestionably his own. He considered not even bothering to separate his gas station glasses, his pots and pans, from the rest of the house-wares, but the collecting and packing eliminated the necessity for conversation. He sets the box by the door; later in the afternoon, his cousin is to come by with a pick-up truck and Richard wants to be able to load everything quickly.

In a corner of the living room, Mrs. Freer wraps Katie's wedding china in newspapers before putting the pieces into boxes. Movers will come in the morning, hired by the Freers to remove Katie's things: the furniture, the washer, the dryer, the freezer, the refrigerator and oven — the amazing accumulation of goods received from her parents — to the Freer home in Dayton. Mrs. Freer's glasses slide down her nose on a float of sweat. Richard supposes that he could turn on the air conditioner (his own shirt sticks to his back, his sneakers are clammy) but he takes a certain guilty pleasure in watching the woman suffer, and he imagines himself undergoing a necessary purification through submission to the heat.

"You want me to move that for you?" he asks Mrs. Freer as she closes a cardboard box.

"Would you?" she says, and points to the pile opposite Richard's own collection of suitcases and boxes. One of the few things he and Katie bought together, a bamboo shade, leans up against Mrs. Freer's pile. Richard hoped to take the shade, but now it is impossible; he would feel as though he were asking Mrs. Freer for something of her own.

He hefts the box of china as Mrs. Freer steps out of the clutter of newspapers and begins rummaging in her purse. The rustle and smell of newsprint make him think of Sunday mornings and he and Katie and Mark going through fat *Tribunes* together. He sets the box down next to Mrs. Freer's pile, allows his fingers to trail along the bamboo shade's hard ribs. The end of one rib is cracked, a slim finger-length break. He works a fingernail into the crack, works the sliver away from the rib. The shade's cheap coat of varnish fractures as the split runs.

"You didn't bring your car, Richard," Mrs. Freer says.

"It's being worked on."

"Nothing serious, I hope."

"No," he says, and, to avoid her eyes, bends to tie his shoelace.

"Well, would you mind taking my car and getting some more boxes?" In one hand, she waves a stiff twenty dollar bill; in the other, she jingles a ring of keys. Richard finishes tying his shoelace, but he does not stand. He looks up at the keys; they are attached to a blue plastic hexagon which reads "Freer Aluminum Products." He studies the bottom half of Mrs. Freer's legs: solid, immense. Nothing like Katie's.

"And while you're gone, you could pick up some lunch. Hamburgers. Or anything you'd like."

In his pocket, he has, perhaps, four dollars. Tonight he'll stay at his cousin's, but he still owes eighteen to the motel, plus the garage.

"I've got money," he says.

* * *

Three times the car turned over. He doesn't want details. The ugly row of stitches — a lunatic ampersand carved into Mark's skull — is more than enough information. Richard reasoned the two of them would need six hours for the trip to Dayton, but he didn't know what time they left for home. He called her parents at one in the morning; he waited that long. A stranger, who identified herself as a neighbor, answered the phone. She didn't know who Richard was. Then Katie's mother was on, saying something so unintelligible that Richard understood immediately.

* * *

He returns with boxes and a bag of french fries, hamburgers, and cokes. At the front door, he pauses, wondering if he might be expected to ring the bell now, then decides that, expected or not, it would be more awkward to explain *why* he rang than to enter unannounced.

The coolness is a surprise; she has turned on the air conditioning.

In the bedroom, Mrs. Freer makes piles of clothing — shirts, shorts, skirts, underwear. She clears her throat. "I guess we could take these to

104

Goodwill," she says. Richard nods, but suspects her of wanting to add them to her own crammed closets; when he visited the Freer home, there wasn't even a place for him to hang his shirts.

He sits on the edge of the mattress, exhausted. Already the room is changed; she's stripped the sheets (discretely covering stains on the mattress with pillows), taken down the curtains, thrown out the plants that died while he stayed at the motel. Behind her, metal hangers tap against one another like delicate, oriental chimes. He wants to ask for the plaid shirt she is folding against her chest, but he doesn't know how to say the words, worries that the request might sound deviant.

Mrs. Freer looks up from her folding and smiles, lips so tight and high her chin seems to acquire length: Katie's smile in moments of extreme self-consciousness. Richard stands, holds up the bag of food. "I got us lunch," he says and hurries back down the hall.

* * *

"These we won't have to wash!" Mrs. Freer says as she sets paper plates on the dining room table.

Richard, who is eating out of a bag, takes the plates as a reproach. "We never used them. Bad for the environment."

"Well, just this once won't hurt."

Richard shifts in his chair; the Lincoln log in his pocket jams into his thigh, a small discomfort he feels he can do nothing about.

"Why don't you take the stereo?" she says.

"Thanks, but I really don't need it," he says quickly.

Katie teased him about his own superior equipment, left at his parents' home in Tulsa: "You're smart not bringing it here, Richard. Who knows? I might just absorb it." Then she brought her face very close to his and laughed a vampire's laugh he didn't think entirely funny.

He says to Mrs. Freer, "You take it. One of the boys might use it."

"Well, all right," she says with a little sigh. "I guess I'll do these things next." She nods her head in the direction of the breakfront housing Katie's knickknacks. "It's hard to know what to save," she says. "There are some good pieces, of course, but I hate to throw out things that were special." Her eyes move over the odd collection of rocks, pine cones, a cloisonne vase, piggy banks. "What's that?" she asks, pointing to a twig studded with eggshells.

"Something Mark made. I'd kind of like to have it if you don't want it."

"Fine, fine." Her eyes wander about the room. She dunks a french fry in ketchup, inspects it, sets it carefully on the edge of her paper plate. "What will you do now, Richard?" she says, voice so plaintive that he winces; it is as if she has said to him, how will you bear it? how will you go on?

"I really don't want to talk about it right now," he says. "No offense, it's just too difficult."

In her lap, she folds and unfolds her napkin, irons the creases with her hand. "I'd just like to know," she says. "We'll be thinking of you."

105

"I'm taking the job in Illinois. I'll be there," he says.

"I'm glad! It's a good school. I'm just so glad." She leans forward in her chair. "And will you let us know how you're doing?"

"Sure," he says. The hidden request both touches and angers him, and he looks away in confusion.

"And you'll try to see Markie, too?"

"Look," he says, "you're talking about Mark. Nobody needs to tell me not to forget Mark."

"Why, Richard, I know you're crazy about Mark! I didn't mean anything at all. I suppose it's just I can't bear to think of that darling little boy ending up with *him*." Like Katie, who dramatized her emotions, she rubs the top of her arms as if cold. "We've got our lawyers looking into it. Unless he can be found incompetent, we haven't got a prayer."

He thinks again of the trip to the grandparents' home in Dayton, the collection of Mark's baby's pictures, the father neatly excised by Mrs. Freer's scissors. "Paul's not incompetent," he says, feeling oddly as if a defense of Paul is somehow a defense of himself.

"How can you be so calm about it? We've lost Mark, just as much as we've lost her!" She takes a bite of her hamburger, then begins to weep, great heaving sobs which move her shoulders up and down.

At the funeral, where the grief was general, there, he could comfort the woman. Here, her tears make him feel helpless and accused. She wipes her eyes with one of the stiff commercial napkins, blows her nose. "If only you'd been married," she says.

"*Please.*" He jabs at the air in front of her face with his index finger, and she sits back in her chair. "I'd have Mark? She'd still be alive? How about if only she hadn't gone to see you? How about that?"

"Oh, Richard, be fair."

He stuffs the empty cups, the odd little boxes for hamburgers and french fries into the bag and he stands. "I didn't kill her," he says, his voice surprising him with its cold theatricality. His heart thumps in his ears. He says, "Try to remember that," only this time the words come out slow, exhausted, send him hurrying away from the woman's pale face and towards the privacy of the bathroom.

* * *

He lathers between his fingers, up his arms. The smell of Katie's pale blue soap is sweet and familiar. He rinses, lathers again, thinks of her sitting down beside him on the front steps. It was late. She wore a nightgown and her hair was wet from the shower. The smell of just-applied perfume rose from her skin, sharp, almost like a man's after shave. She said, "Do you ever do this? Do you ever pick out something to remember?"

"Why?" he said. They had quarrelled earlier and he half-resented her breaking their silence.

"Because, most of the time you don't get to choose at al!. I've forgotten so much I shouldn't have and ended up remembering the ashtrays in the orthodontist's."

"And?"

She took a great breath. "I just was thinking we should be choosy," she said, and leaned her head on his shoulder. "Particularly about each other."

Forgiving her was easy. They kissed as she jumped up from the steps and danced out onto the lawn. "Aren't I wild?" she cried. "On Bradley Street in my nightgown?"

She knew two steps of the Highland Fling, and lifting her gown to her knees, did them over and over again, winter-white legs scissoring faster and faster in the dark.

* * *

He tries to roll the bar of soap in his hands, but it is too thin; he rubs it between his palms, feeling it wear away into lather.

"Richard?" Mrs. Freer says from outside the bathroom door. He turns the water off. "Richard?"

"Yes."

She clears her throat. "I'd like to speak to you, if I could," she says.

Richard sticks his head out the door. By not stepping out into the hallway he can keep the conversation short. He rubs his head with towel, as if he has just finished washing his hair. Mrs. Freer smiles.

"I have something for you," she says.

In her hand, she holds a check. Richard reads his name, the figure. One thousand dollars and zero one-hundredths. She reaches for his arm, but he steps back into the bathroom.

"Please. You'll need it. It will help you get a start. Please, take it for me."

He sees himself crumple the check into a ball, imagines the dry click of its hitting her cheek, but then what? He slides his back down the wall until he's seated on his haunches. He breathes deeply, trying to calm himself.

"She was my *baby*, Richard," she says, and then more softly, "She was my little girl." She bends over and places the check on his kneecap. "She loved you and you loved her."

The check wafts from his knee and onto the floor. It is one of those contemporary designs: pale pink paper, hearty cardinals flying across its center, the sort of thing he and Katie would laugh over. He and Katie used gray checks. Gray checks with black print.

He folds birds and all in half, stands. Mrs. Freer nods encouragement with small, tired bobs of her head.

"Thank you," he says, "Thank you very much."

An ugly noise — like the shudder of old and failing pipes — rises from deep inside him; and he finds that in all the world, there is one comfort left: to be held in those heavy arms while she rubs his back with the flat of her hand and whispers, "Sh, sh, there, there."